Peril at the Beach

Suddenly—

"OWWWWW!!"

Bess and I whirled around to see George hopping up and down on one foot.

"George, what happened?" I asked.

George clutched her other ankle. "I stepped on something sharp. It went underneath my sandal and pricked the side of my foot."

"Maybe a jellyfish stung you," Bess said.

Bess could be right, I thought. But when I saw a stream of bright red blood beneath George's ankle, I changed my mind.

"That's no sting," I decided.

"Well, it was either that soda can ring, broken glass," George said, her face turning ghost white, "or . . . or . . ."

"Or what?" I asked.

"Or that hypodermic needle?" George gulped.

NANCY DREW

Available from Aladdin

CAROLYN KEENE

NANCY DREW

GIRL DETECTIVE®

California Schemin'

#45

**Book One in the
Malibu Mayhem Trilogy**

Aladdin

New York London Toronto Sydney

✿ALADDIN
An imprint of Simon & Schuster Children's Publishing Division
1230 Avenue of the Americas, New York, NY 10020
First Aladdin paperback edition June 2011
Copyright © 2011 by Simon & Schuster, Inc.
All rights reserved, including the right of
reproduction in whole or in part in any form.
ALADDIN is a trademark of Simon & Schuster, Inc., and related logo is a registered trademark of Simon & Schuster, Inc.
NANCY DREW, NANCY DREW: GIRL DETECTIVE, and related logo are registered trademarks of Simon & Schuster, Inc.
For information about special discounts for bulk purchases, please contact Simon & Schuster Special Sales at 1-866-506-1949
or business@simonandschuster.com.
The Simon & Schuster Speakers Bureau can bring authors to your live event.
For more information or to book an event contact the Simon & Schuster Speakers Bureau at 1-866-248-3049 or visit our website at www.simonspeakers.com.
Designed by Karina Granda
The text of this book was set in Bembo.
Manufactured in the United States of America 0414 OFF
10 9 8 7 6 5 4
Library of Congress Control Number 2011921046
ISBN 978-1-4424-2295-7
ISBN 978-1-4424-2296-4 (eBook)

Contents

SUNSET SHOCKER

"Girls," I said, smiling between smoothie sips. "I don't think we're in River Heights anymore."

"For sure," George said. She raised her own raspberry smoothie glass and toasted, "To Malachite Beach!"

"Playground of the rich and famous," Bess piped up. "And now . . . us."

Leaning forward, I clinked glasses with my BFFs, Bess Marvin and George Fayne. The three of us were lounging on a deck overlooking the most awesome moonlit beach we had ever seen in our lives.

We'd been in Malachite for only a few hours, but I still wanted to pinch myself to see if I was dreaming. Having the run of a California beach house for three weeks was a dream come true.

George leaned back in her chair to prop her sandy feet on the deck's railing. The first thing she'd done when we got to the house was kick off her sneakers and race down to the beach. Our own *private* beach.

"Do I know people in the right places or what?" George asked with a grin. "Who can say their mom worked with Stacey Manning, event planner to the stars?"

"Only you, George," I teased. "And only about a hundred times."

Bess scrunched her nose as she studied George's feet. "How about saying 'pedicure'?"

I laughed as George wiggled her feet in front of a horrified Bess's face. Our dream vacation was going to be a blast, thanks to Stacey.

Stacey Manning was truly an event planner extraordinaire. She planned parties and events for some of the hottest celebrities in Hollywood and all over the country.

"Did you read about the Sweet Sixteen Stacey threw for those celebrity twins?" I asked. "The one aboard an actual refurbished pirate ship?"

"You mean the party where each guest left with a full-size treasure chest filled with swag?" Bess asked.

"Some swag," George snorted. "I read online that those treasure chests were packed with MP3 players, diamond charm bracelets, and cameras."

"Don't forget the gift cards," Bess added. "To the hottest restaurants in Hollywood."

"MP3 players, diamond charms, and cameras?" I said. "Now I *know* we're not in River Heights anymore."

The three of us stopped talking to watch the setting of a deep orange sun. As it slowly sank behind the ocean, I thought of my boyfriend, Ned, back in River Heights, wishing he was at my side. But as much as I missed Ned, I wouldn't trade this awesome getaway for anything. Even detectives like us needed a little vacay now and then.

"Hey, George," Bess asked. "Did Stacey lend us this epic house just because she worked with your mom?"

"Not really," George said. "Offering us the house was Stacey's way of thanking my mom. When Stacey goofed up during an event years ago, my mom covered for her."

"Really?" I said, surprised. "I can't imagine Stacey goofing up any party."

"What did she do?" Bess wanted to know.

"Her first day on the job, Stacey placed an ice sculpture next to the flambé station," George said. "The sculpture had a meltdown, and so did their boss."

"Not a good way to start a job," I said.

"Was Stacey fired?" Bess asked.

"She might have been if Mom hadn't taken the blame," George explained. "Mom always had a soft spot for newbies."

She stretched back lazily in her chair before adding, "Mom hadn't heard from Stacey in years. So she was totally surprised when Stacey called last week."

"Better late than never," I said, smiling.

Stacey had given us the use of not only her house, but her car, private beach, and a stocked fridge.

But as cool as our temporary Malachite house was, we were in California—and that meant places to go and things to see.

"Don't forget, you guys," I reminded. "I want to do all the touristy stuff while we're here. Universal Studios, Venice Beach—"

"Rodeo Drive," Bess cut in. She flipped her long blond hair over her shoulder and smiled. "We have to do Rodeo Drive as soon as possible."

George rolled her eyes at the mention of L.A.'s famous and *expensive* shopping district.

"Bess," George complained. "Stacey Manning left us her house. Not her credit cards."

4

"Okay, Miss Low Maintenance." Bess sighed. "What do *you* plan to do—stare at a computer all day, as usual?"

"Actually," George said, turning toward the ocean, "I'd like to go surfing."

Surfing was definitely on my list. Especially since Stacey had left us three new boards.

"Maybe I'll tag along, George," I decided.

"While you work the California waves," Bess said, "I'll work on my California tan."

Tan? I stared at Bess as if she had three heads. "Bess, you know baking in the sun can be dangerous, even with globs of sunscreen on."

This time Bess stared at *me* as if I had three heads.

"*Sunless spray-tanning*," Bess pronounced the words carefully. "Remember, this is L.A."

It sure was. As I glanced up at the darkening Los Angeles sky, even the stars seemed brighter. And speaking of stars . . .

"Do you think we'll see any major celebs while we're in Malachite?" I asked.

"Hope so." Bess smiled.

"Not me," George said before taking a noisy slurp of her smoothie. "Who cares about celebrities unless they invented Facebook or Twitter?"

Bess stood up and leaned over the railing. She twisted her head to check out the houses along the beach.

"Maybe, just maybe," she said slowly, "some of those famous celebrities are living near us."

Bess could have been right. Stacey's house wasn't as huge or grand as the other mansions or villas. But it was on the most famous star-studded beach in the world.

"I'm not sure of our other neighbors," I said. "But that mansion right next door seems to be some kind of spa."

Bess spun around. "Did you say spa?" she demanded. "How do you know there's a spa next door?"

"I read the sign as our taxi drove by," I said. "It said something like 'Roland's Renewal Retreat and Spa.'"

"Talk about having a photographic memory," George said, smiling at me. "I'm impressed."

"So am I—about the spa," Bess said excitedly. "You guys, we have to go there at least once for mani-pedis."

"As if I'm the spa type," George scoffed. "What would I need a manicure for?"

"For starters"—Bess picked up George's hand—"they can probably scrape those calluses off your fingertips. The ones you get from all that keyboarding."

"Keyboard" was George's magic word, as was any word that had to do with computers—which is why it was still so hard to believe Bess and George were cousins. Not only did they look totally different, everything they did and liked was as different as Malachite Beach and River Heights.

Bess, George, and I hung out on Stacey's deck until the cool Santa Ana winds made us shiver.

"Time to go inside," I said, standing up.

"I'm coming too." Bess pulled out her phone and checked the time. "I have to catch my favorite guilty pleasure on TV."

"Who cares about TV when we're on vacation?" George asked.

"Me," Bess replied. "There's no way I'm going to miss *Chillin' with the Casabians*."

I shuddered but not from the cool night air. I knew *Chillin' with the Casabians* was a reality show about three super-glam sisters famous for being famous. I also knew from experience that reality shows were bad news.

"Oh, Bess, wasn't being on *Daredevils* bad enough?" I groaned.

"Yeah," George said. "We almost got killed working on that case—and being on that show."

But Bess shook her head and smiled.

"*Chillin' with the Casabians* isn't like *Daredevils*. It's good, goofy fun," she insisted. "And you just never know what Mandy, Mallory, or Mia will do—or wear—next."

"Or what *dumb* thing they'll *say*," George said.

"Does that mean you're going to watch *Chillin' with the Casabians* with me?" Bess teased George.

"I'm going on Stacey's computer," George said. "I'm pretty sure I can make it run even faster than it already does."

I stopped in my tracks to stare at George.

"Excuse me, Queen of the Cyberzons," I joked. "But we're on vacation, and vacation means no work. Period."

Bess cast a sly glance my way. "No work?" she asked. "Does that mean no mysteries, either?"

Good question. But as much as I loved solving all kinds of mysteries, I also loved having a little time off.

"No mysteries," I said firmly. "I don't know about you, but this girl detective is hanging up her spyglass for this vacation."

"You might as well." George shrugged. "What's the worst thing that could happen in a place like this?"

Bess pointed to her wind-whipped hair and said, "A bad hair day?"

I gazed out at the moonlit waves rolling gently onto the beach. Bess and George were right. Malachite Beach was nothing but peaceful and serene. No wonder celebrities and millionaires called it home. Who wouldn't want to live in such a perfect place? But just as I was about to turn toward the door—

FLASH!!

"Omigod!" I gasped as bright red flames shot up on the beach. "You guys—our beach is on fire!"

UNINVITED GUESTS

"**H**ow can a beach be on fire?" George asked. But when she saw the flames, her dark eyes popped wide open. "Whoa! Somebody must have tossed a cigarette butt on some driftwood."

"Call the fire department," I said, trying hard to stay calm.

"On it," Bess said, digging into her pocket. "I'll text 911."

"Don't text, call!" I said, feeling my heart pounding in my chest.

George leaned against the railing for a closer look.

She then spun around and grabbed Bess's arm just as she was about to press the last digit.

"Don't!" George told Bess.

"Why not?" Bess cried.

"Because it's not that kind of fire," George said quickly.

Bess and I turned toward the flames still shooting up from the sand.

"Um, flames . . . smoke?" I said.

"Looks like a fire to me," Bess insisted.

"It *is* a fire," George explained. "A *bonfire*."

Bess and I looked again. Squinting, I made out four silhouettes sitting on blankets near the fire. The bonfire.

"You're right!" Bess smiled with relief as she pocketed her phone.

"But this is Stacey's beach. Her *private* beach," George reminded us.

She was right. A private beach meant no trespassing. And setting up a bonfire on private property was definitely trespassing.

"Come on," I said, waving my hand in the direction of the beach. "We'd better find out who's down there."

Bess, George, and I climbed down from the deck and walked across the sand toward the bonfire crackling near the shore. As we got closer, the four figures came into view—two girls and two guys, probably in their late teens or early twenties. The girls had long, dark hair and were wearing hoodies. Not your typical sweatshirt hoodies, but ones studded with crystals and trimmed with faux fur. Two picnic baskets overflowed with breads, fruit, and drinks.

We stopped about ten feet from the fire. The partyers were shrieking playfully as flaming embers shot in their direction.

"Stiletto-heeled boots?" I whispered as one girl kicked her feet in the air. "On the beach?"

"Yeah, but check *them* out," Bess said about the guys, who had long, layered hair. "They're total hunks, no matter what they're wearing."

"Who cares what they look like?" George said. "They're still partying on a private beach. Who do they think they are?"

Bess shook my arm as she gave a little gasp. "I think I know who they are," she said. "But it's too dark to be sure."

A bright light flashed in the corner of my eye. I turned to see a woman wearing a ball cap and carrying a clipboard rushing toward the bonfire. Stumbling behind her were two guys, both wearing backward caps. One held a TV camera on his shoulder. The other gripped a dangling mike.

"They're filming something?" I wondered out loud. "On the beach?"

"Listen up, everybody!" the woman called to the group. "I want Mandy and Mallory to argue over who forgot the marshmallows. Then we'll do a one-shot of Mandy complaining how Mallory always forgets everything."

"Who *says* I forget everything?" one of the girls argued. "Why do I always have to be the airhead, Bev?"

"Because you are?" the other girl teased.

"It is them," Bess hissed excitedly. "It's Mandy and Mallory Casabian. The guys are their boyfriends, Devon and Ty."

"Casabian?" George asked. "From *Chillin' with the Casabians*?"

"What a coincidence, right?" Bess whispered. "Mandy is the oldest and a total know-it-all. Devon and Ty are surfers and aspiring Abercrombie models. Devon already greets customers at the door."

I cast a disgusted glance Bess's way. The last thing I wanted in our own backyard was a reality show. Especially after what we'd gone through on *Daredevils* not long ago.

"Bess, it's a reality show. Those girls are the furthest things from reality I can think of," I said.

"I don't care who they are," George said in a much louder voice. She began walking ahead of us toward the bonfire. "Even if they were the March sisters from *Little Women*—they still can't trespass on private property."

"George, wait!" Bess called as she hurried after her cousin. I was about to do the same when I was blinded by the camera lights.

"Hey!" As I shaded my eyes with my hand, I saw Bev walking toward us.

"Whoever said that line about *Little Women*," Bev said, her eyes darting from me to Bess to George, "can you repeat it to Mandy and Mallory so I can get it on camera?"

"So are we still rolling, Bev?" the cameraman asked.

"What do they pay you for, Wayne?" Bev shouted. "Of course we're rolling."

"We are *not* rolling!" I snapped. Making the universal throat-slashing signal with my hand, I began shouting, "Cut! Cut! Cut!"

"Excuse me, Red," Bev yelled, charging toward me. "Only the director is allowed to say 'cut.'"

"Union rule." Wayne nodded.

"Nancy's hair is strawberry blond," George said. "And I have a rule too. No trespassing on my private beach."

By now the sisters and their boyfriends were openly gaping at us.

"Your beach?" Mallory asked. Her hair swung back and forth as she shook her head. "Nuh-uh. This is Stacey Manning's beach."

"We thought Stacey was still away," Mandy said coolly. "She is, isn't she?"

"How do *you* know Stacey Manning?" I asked.

The sisters traded looks as if to say, *Du-uh*. Then they turned back to us.

"We live next door," Mandy said. "Our sister Mia didn't want us making noise on our own beach, so we came here. She is such a drag."

"Stacey *is* away on business," George explained. "But she put us in charge of her house and her beach. That means—"

"Wait a minute, did you say next door?" Bess asked the sisters. "Does that mean we're staying right next to Villa Fabuloso?"

"Villa Fabuloso?" George repeated.

"The one and only," Mandy said in a bored voice. A tiny Yorkshire terrier hopped out of her beach bag. The Yorkie wagged his tail at us and barked.

"Peanut Butter!" Bess declared. "Hi, Peanut."

This time I rolled my eyes. I always knew Bess was starstruck. But this was more like being struck hard on the head with a star-studded mallet.

Waving my friends away from the blanket, I murmured, "Meeting."

"What's up?" Bess whispered. "You said you wanted to meet some celebs in Hollywood. Remember?"

"Yeah, I remember," I whispered back. "But I

don't want to be in another reality show. Ever."

"And I promised Stacey I'd take care of her beach," George said in a voice louder than a whisper. "That means no intruders, celebrities or not."

"Oh, come on, George," Bess urged. "Let's let the sisters and their boyfriends stay on the beach, at least tonight."

With a little shrug, she added, "And who knows? We may even get to chill with the Casabians."

"Not if it means being on another reality show," I insisted.

"I'm telling them to pack up," George said. She started walking forward until Bess grabbed her arm.

"George, for all we know Stacey and the sisters are friends," Bess said. "You wouldn't want to spoil their relationship, would you?"

"How do we know they're good neighbors?" George demanded.

"We don't," Bess said. "But are you willing to take that chance?"

George stopped walking. Her shoulders dropped before she finally said, "Okay. They can stay, but just tonight."

"And no cameras on us," I added.

The three of us walked past Bev to the blanket.

"You can stay on the beach tonight," George told them. "Just don't make a lot of noise, because we're still jet-lagged. Make sure you clean up and take everything with you when you leave."

"Yes, ma'am!" Mandy said, pretending to salute.

"And please don't film us without our permission," I said, giving Bev a sideways glance.

"Whoa!" Ty stood up and ran his fingers through his hair. "Did you say you're jet-lagged? Like, where are you guys from?"

"River Heights," Bess said with a smile. "It's in the Midwest."

"The Midwest?" Devon piped up. "You mean like near Santa Cruz?"

"Give me a break," I could hear George say under her breath.

"River Heights is in the Midwest—of America," Bess started to explain. "Right near—"

"Places, everybody!" Bev shouted, making us jump. "Let's pick up with the marshmallow issue. Mandy, I want you to really want those marshmallows!"

"But I hate marshmallows," Mandy whined. "So many carbs."

"I hate *this*," I whispered to Bess and George. "Let's go back. Please?"

We left the sisters and their show behind as we made our way back to the house.

"What's the other sister, Mia, like?" George asked. "Is she anything like Mindy and Valerie?"

"Mandy and Mallory!" Bess corrected. "Mia's the complete opposite. She's the youngest and considered the plain one, even though she's really cute."

"Bess, you know way too much about these girls," George said.

"I'm not finished about Mia," said Bess. "Mandy and Mallory are always trying to give Mia a makeover, but Mia would rather hang out in sweats and actually read a good book."

"In that case," I said with a smile, "I think I like Mia best."

"Oh, Mia is the brainy one, all right," Bess agreed. "But as the other sisters say, what good are brains if nobody sees them?"

"You're kidding me, right?" George cried. "Bess, you're out of control."

She ran up the steps of the deck and into the house. Bess and I stopped on the deck to shake the sand off our flip-flops.

"Admit it, Nance," Bess said as she tapped her flip-flop on the railing. "Meeting stars in Hollywood is a lot more exciting than polar bears in Antarctica."

"I don't know about that," I replied. "But it is kind of cool having celebrities right next door. Even if they *are* reality stars."

Bess playfully swung a flip-flop at me while we crossed the deck into the house. I could hear Mandy shouting something about marshmallows as I closed the door and locked up.

Bess turned on the last few minutes of *Chillin'* *with the Casabians*, still excited to have met them. George was too tired to work on Stacey's computer. My jet lag was kicking in too, so I said good night and headed to the guest room I had picked when we arrived.

It didn't take long for me to fall asleep in the huge four-poster bed with squishy down pillows and comforters. But sometime in the middle of the night I was awakened by the sound of voices. Singing voices from outside.

The room was still dark. I looked at the clock on the night table. Three thirty a.m.! What was going on?

"Are they going to party all night?" I groaned to myself. I wrapped a pillow around my head and ears. Luckily, it was as thick as it was soft, so I had no trouble falling back to sleep.

Early the next morning I woke up to the California sun shining through the sheer white curtains. I was ready to start my first full day in L.A. We'd start the day with a short run, then decide what else to do.

"Let's run along the water," Bess suggested as we climbed down from the deck onto the beach. "This way we can check out the other houses."

"And more celebrities?" I teased.

"Well, I'm ready for anything today," George said. "I slept like a log."

"Not me," I admitted. "Well, at least not the whole night."

"How come?" Bess asked. She used the hem of her T-shirt to wipe a smudge off her sunglasses.

"I heard some kind of singing that woke me up at three thirty in the morning," I explained.

"Singing?" Bess asked, slipping on her shades.

"Or some kind of chanting coming from outside," I said. "My room faces the beach, so it was probably the Casabians and their boyfriends. Our luck we have to have a reality show filming right next door."

"I told those sisters to keep the noise down and to clean up." George was livid.

"You also told them it would be their last night on the beach," I reminded her. "So let's just forget it."

George sighed as we began jogging toward the water. "You're right," she said. "Why should a bunch of Hollywood airheads ruin my vacation?"

"George!" Bess complained.

But as we neared the water, we froze in our tracks. The bonfire, beach blankets, and picnic baskets were gone.

In its place was trash—*tons of it!*

SHORE DISASTER

We stared at the mess, too shocked to speak. Finally George said, "Do you believe what they did to Stacey's beach?"

"Gross," Bess said, shaking her head.

I was appalled too as I gazed at a sea of aluminum cans, plastic bottles, sandwich crusts, even empty makeup containers.

"Not only is it disgusting," I pointed out, "most of this stuff is probably toxic and dangerous to the environment."

To prove my point, I picked up a plastic six-pack holder. "Some poor gull can get his neck caught in one of these," I explained. "Or swallow a ring from one of those soda cans."

"I don't get it," George said. "I thought Hollywood celebrities were all about being green these days. I mean, even their pets eat organic foods."

"Can you believe this?" Bess said. "Our first full day of vacation and it's already interrupted."

"Thanks to Mandy and Mallory," I said. "I told you I didn't want to have anything to do with this show."

"Well, those sisters are about to hear from us," George said. "It's time to pay a little visit to this Villa Fabuloso."

George pulled out her phone to snap a picture of the trash. "Just in case they need to be reminded," she huffed.

I could see by Bess's face that she was worried. Probably about upsetting her television idols.

"George is right, Bess," I told her. "If the sisters dumped the trash, then they have to own up to it, and clean it up."

"But what if this is a setup for their TV show?" Bess asked. "What if they left the trash on the beach on purpose? So we would go over there and make a scene?"

"Oh, wow," I said. "I never thought of that."

"I don't care why the trash is here," George said. "Just that it *is* here."

George started toward Villa Fabuloso, glanced over her shoulder, and said, "Coming with me?"

"Why not?" Bess sighed. "Even if we're humiliated, I'll get to see Villa Fabuloso."

I decided to go too. If there was a camera crew waiting for us, I'd deal with it. The sisters' house was accessible only by walking along the beach. I felt security cameras eyeing us as we turned onto the sugary-white beach of Villa Fabuloso.

"Funny," George said with a hint of sarcasm. "*Their* beach isn't trashed."

She was right. All I could see were striped beach chairs and an unattended refreshment bar.

"This place is exactly like its name," Bess swooned as we followed a stone path from the beach to the house. "Fabulous."

It sure was. The sisters' three-story house looked more like a mansion, with massive white pillars flanking the front entrance. The scent of exotic flowers wafted to my nose as we passed a lush garden surrounding a stone fountain.

"Where do you think the swimming pool is?" I asked.

"Which one?" George snorted.

We stepped up to a pink front door. On it was a heart-shaped brass door knocker. George chose to ring the doorbell instead.

"Oh, fun." Bess giggled. "The bell plays the theme song from *Chillin' with the Casabians*."

I gritted my teeth as the door swung open, expecting to be blinded by camera lights. Instead the door was opened by a middle-aged woman wearing a crisp white uniform.

I glanced over her shoulder into the house. No camera. No lights. No director. Whew!

"Good morning," she said with a big smile. "What can I do for you?"

I smiled back at the woman I guessed was the housekeeper. Seeing her made me miss our own housekeeper, Hannah Gruen. Ever since my mom died when I was three, Hannah had been more like a mother to me than a housekeeper. She always wore comfy pantsuits and dresses, never a uniform.

"Good morning," I said. "We're guests of Stacey Manning next door, and we'd like to see Mandy and Mallory."

The housekeeper glanced at the six-pack holder still in my hand and said, "I'm afraid Mandy and Mallory are still asleep."

"Too much partying last night?" George asked before Bess gave her a swift elbow jab.

"I heard that," a voice piped up.

The housekeeper stepped away from the door to make room for Mandy, still in pajama pants, a cami, and fuzzy slippers. I couldn't help but notice how much prettier she looked without gobs of makeup.

"Ursula, can you make a full pot of coffee, please?" Mandy croaked, her voice still raspy from sleep.

"Certainly," Ursula said, and quickly left.

Mandy blinked her sleepy eyes at us.

"So . . . what's up?" she asked.

George pulled out her phone and waved the picture she'd taken in front of Mandy's face.

"This is what's up," George declared. "We woke up this morning to a ton of trash on Stacey's beach."

Mandy blinked at the picture, yawned, then murmured, "Really?"

I stared at Mandy in disbelief. Not only was she careless—she was callous!

"Yeah, really," I said, holding up the six-pack holder. "We told you guys to pick up your things before you left last night."

"Our crew picked up everything," Mandy insisted. "At least that's what they were doing when Mallory and I left the beach last night."

"They did?" Bess asked.

Mandy yawned again. She continued, "Mallory and I didn't stay much longer after you left. Just long enough to tape the marshmallow scene and that's it."

I remembered the singing I'd heard early this morning. Was that what they called not staying late?

"What time did you leave?" I asked, cocking my head.

"What are you—some kind of detectives?" Mandy asked. "It was right before midnight, since we had some serious clubbing to do. The Bill E. Boyz were promoting their new CD on Sunset."

Was Mandy for real? Or was this clubbing excuse just some made-up alibi?

"If you guys didn't leave the garbage on the beach last night," I asked, "then who did?"

Mandy groaned under her breath. "Look, I don't have time to argue," she said. "I have to eat breakfast before the crew gets here."

Bess was looking past Mandy into the house. "Do you think we can meet Mia?" she asked with a smile. Leave it to Bess—she never gives up.

I was surprised to see Mandy's face drop at the mention of Mia. "You'll have to go to Roland's Renewal Retreat and Spa for that."

"You mean the spa at the end of the beach?" Bess asked. "I thought Mia wasn't into spas. What's she doing there?"

"Mallory and I sent Mia to the spa a few weeks ago, for the complete makeover," Mandy said.

"Another brilliant idea for your show?" George asked.

"No, I'm afraid not," Mandy answered. "The

Renewal Retreat doesn't allow cameras, not even personal ones. It wasn't easy getting Mia to go," she went on. "She finally went over for the full-day package."

"How did she like it?" Bess asked.

"Well, she *must* have liked it." Mandy frowned. "The full-day package turned into a few weeks."

"Wait a minute," I said, trying to understand. "You mean she's *still* at the spa?"

Mandy nodded, and then—

"I need coffeeeeeee!" another voice shouted from upstairs. "Somebody make a humongous pot, please. The extra-strong kind!"

"It's already on, Mallory!" Mandy yelled up the stairs. She turned back to us with what seemed like a fake smile. "And don't worry, because we won't be partying on your beach anymore."

"But what about the garbage?" I asked. "You're the only ones—"

"Buh-bye," Mandy cut in before shutting the door in our faces. We stood staring at it for a few seconds before turning and walking away.

"So what do you think?" George asked as we walked away from the door. "Was Mandy telling the truth about the trash or what?"

I tried to remember everything Mandy had told us. What time they left the beach, where they'd gone.

"The noises I heard were way after midnight," I pointed out. "If Mandy lied about when they left, she could be lying about the trash, too. I don't trust them."

"If only we could ask Mallory some questions," Bess said. "After her coffee, of course."

"We don't have to bother," George said as we turned onto our own beach. "I'm pretty sure Mandy lied and that the sisters are guilty as charged."

I was pretty sure they were too. But it was no use crying over dumped trash.

"It's still our beach, at least for now," I said. "Let's clean it ourselves and get it over with so we can start our vacation."

"Then Rodeo Drive!" Bess declared with a smile.

"I think I'd rather pick up trash," George joked. "But not with our bare hands. Maybe Stacey has some work gloves we can wear."

"Let's check the shed over there," I said, pointing to a small wooden hut near the side of the house.

As we headed toward the shed, I remembered what Mandy had said about Mia.

"How can Mia go to a spa for a day and end up staying for weeks?" I wondered.

"Maybe she wanted to get away from her sisters," George said.

"Or maybe she decided she likes being pampered from head to toe," Bess said.

George rolled her eyes. "Another Hollywood princess. Just what this town needs."

As we approached the shed, I smiled when I saw the three surfboards leaning against the outside. I couldn't wait to surf some real Malachite waves. Or at least try to.

"Check out all those tools," Bess said when we opened the door. Wrenches, screwdrivers, and drills hung on the walls. "Imagine all the things I could fix and build."

"How about a robot to clean up the beach?" I joked.

We searched the shed, only to find more tools, a shovel, a lawn mower, and some folded beach chairs. But then George found something in the back that caught her eye: a black wet suit hanging from a hook on the wall.

"I didn't think Stacey was the deep-diving type," George said.

"She must be." I pointed to an oxygen tank, goggles, and flippers underneath the suit on the floor. "She's got all the gear."

"Maybe one of her fabulous parties was under the sea," Bess suggested.

After exploring a little more, we found what we were looking for: a box filled with canvas work gloves, and a roll of jumbo garbage bags.

"We're all set," I said. "Now let's hit the beach and get to work."

The three of us carried our cleanup gear to the trash pile on the beach. As we picked up junk, we couldn't believe what the sisters had left behind: empty face cream containers, used makeup compacts, lipsticks, nail files, and cotton balls, along with empty cans, bottles, and gross stuff like chicken bones, browned and soggy lettuce leaves—even used dental floss. Gross.

"How can four people make such a mess?" Bess said. "They must have invited some friends after we went to bed."

"It sure sounded like more than four people last night," I agreed. "Those Casabians better not ruin this vacation for us. We hardly ever go away."

But as I picked up an empty nail polish bottle, I noticed something else. All the makeup containers seemed to have something in common: a yellow sunburst design on the package.

"It looks like some kind of brand logo," I said, pointing it out to Bess and George. "It's on half of these bottles and jars."

"I've never seen that brand before," Bess admitted. "Whatever it is, the sisters must really like it."

"Eureka!" George joked. "Step aside, famous archeologists of the world. We've just dug up the Casabian sisters' beauty secrets."

I picked up a handful of makeup containers and dropped them into a plastic bag. "Why would Mandy and Mallory need so many beauty products at a bonfire?" I wondered.

"Nancy, there's not a mystery everywhere you look," Bess teased. "The sisters were filming a TV show. They have to be ready for their close-ups at all times."

We stopped cleaning to gaze at the spa. Guests were meditating on the beach. A huge yacht was anchored about two hundred feet from the shore.

"I wonder who that belongs to," I said.

"It's probably for the guests," George replied.

"Or it could belong to that guy Roland who owns the spa," Bess figured. "Business must be good."

There was one more thing on the beach that caught my eye. It was a large tarplike tent covered with thick blankets. "That's a weird-looking tent," I said, pointing it out. "What do you think it's for?"

"Camping? Parties?" Bess shrugged.

"Covered with blankets?" I wondered.

Suddenly—

"OWWWWW!!"

Bess and I whirled around to see George hopping up and down on one foot.

"George, what happened?" I asked.

George clutched her other ankle. "I stepped on

something sharp. It went underneath my sandal and pricked the side of my foot."

"Maybe a jellyfish stung you," Bess said.

Bess could be right, I thought. But when I saw a stream of bright red blood beneath George's ankle, I changed my mind.

"That's no sting," I decided.

"Well, it was either that soda can ring, broken glass," George said, her face turning ghost white, "or . . . or . . ."

"Or what?" I asked.

"Or that hypodermic needle?" George gulped.

TOXIC TROUBLE

My blood froze as I stared at the hypodermic needle sticking halfway out of the sand. It still contained some kind of liquid, which worried me the most. What if it was toxic? What if it went straight into George's bloodstream?

"George, do you really think it was that needle you stepped on?" I asked her.

"I don't know," she answered. "I guess it could have been any of those sharp things."

"We have to get to a hospital, just in case," I said. "Fast!"

Bess shared my panic. She held on to George to

keep her from fainting. "I'll help you to the car," she told her cousin. "Lean on me and keep hopping."

"I'm hopping, I'm hopping," George declared. She leaned on Bess, then hopped alongside her as they made their way up the beach.

"I'll be right there," I yelled as I pulled off my sweatshirt. "I want to bring this with us to the hospital."

"What for?" George called over her shoulder.

"So the doctors can send it to a lab for testing," I answered.

I wrapped my sweatshirt several times around my hand, even though I still had gloves on, almost up to my elbow. Then, very carefully, I scooped up the needle and some surrounding sand into a garbage bag.

Holding the bag out in front of me, I made my way up the beach and around the house to the driveway.

"Hurry up, let's go!" Bess said as I slid into the driver's seat. She had already entered the address of the nearest hospital on the GPS. George sat silently in the backseat as I followed the directions.

"This is not funny," I said as I drove. "Who would think the Casabian sisters could be doing drugs?"

"Unless they're plastic surgery fillers," Bess said. "Let's face it. Those sisters are pretty augmented."

"Can we please shut up about the Casabian sisters

and get me to the hospital?" George cried.

"Turn right at the next light," the perky GPS voice said as I steered the car away from the house. "Then proceed a quarter of a mile."

"Jeez," George grumbled. "What a way to start a vacation!"

Malachite General was only ten minutes away from the house. Bess helped George through the emergency room doors while I followed, the bagged hypodermic needle in hand.

"Please let it only be Botox," I whispered to myself.

A woman behind the desk wasted no time taking George's medical information. A physician's assistant soon joined George to check out her cut.

I knew Bess was worried about George when she didn't flirt with the cute PA. I was worried too. George might not have been my cousin, but she was still one of my two best friends.

"So what do you think I stepped on?" George asked. She tilted her head to read the doctor's name tag. "Dr. Viola?"

"Was it a hypodermic needle?" Bess asked, her voice cracking.

"I don't think it was a needle," Dr. Viola said. "But I'll have to examine it closer to know for sure."

"You can tell just by looking at the cut?" George asked.

"Most of the time," the doctor said with a reassuring smile.

"Well, just in case it was the needle—and we hope it isn't," I said, holding up the garbage bag, "I brought it in for testing."

"That . . . and the whole beach," George blurted.

"Huh?" I glanced down and felt my cheeks burn. Pouring out of a tiny rip in the bag was a steady stream of sand.

"Oops," I groaned.

"Hey, this *is* Malachite Beach." Dr. Viola chuckled. "But you did the right thing by bringing it in. We'll send it to the lab for testing and let you know the results."

Dr. Viola and a nurse helped George into one of the examining rooms. Bess and I found two empty chairs in the waiting room and sat down.

Bess grabbed a fashion magazine from the table and quickly flipped through it. After a few seconds, she tossed it aside.

"Nancy, what if the stuff in the needle was toxic?" Bess asked. "George is my cousin—even if nobody believes it."

"George is in good hands, Bess," I assured her. "Although now I think we should have covered our hands *and* our feet when we were cleaning up."

"It was an accident." Bess sighed. "A terrible accident."

But deep down inside, I wondered. What if the needle on the beach was no accident at all? What if it had been left there on purpose?

"Bess?" I asked slowly. "I hate to bring this up now, but what if Mandy and Mallory left that needle on the beach to provoke us?"

"*Provoke* us?" Bess repeated.

"You know," I said. "To get back at us for giving them a hard time when we found them on our beach?"

"Well, if it *was* meant to hurt one of us," Bess said, "they succeeded."

I was about to grab a news magazine when someone shouted, "Somebody help. Please!"

Bess and I turned in the direction of the voice. A woman who looked about thirty was helping a younger guy through the door. His face was pale, yet beaded with sweat.

"Hang in there, Brad," the woman said.

"I'm . . . okay," the guy panted as he leaned on the woman. "Let's go back, Danielle. Please."

Bess and I watched as a doctor hurried over. She shone what looked like a penlight into his open mouth.

"I'm Dr. Wainwright," she said, her brows furrowed with concern. Do you know what happened?"

I was curious myself. But instead of answering

37

the doctor, the two of them exchanged silent glances.

"Do you have any idea?" Dr. Wainwright asked again.

"Um . . . too much sun?" Danielle answered.

"We'll see," Dr. Wainwright said. She helped Brad into a chair. "You'll need to fill out some forms at the desk while I find an examining room. It shouldn't take long."

The doctor walked past me and Bess.

"Can too much sun do that?" Bess whispered.

"Not according to the doctor," I murmured.

What struck me as weird was how reluctant they were to answer. As if they had something to hide. As if they—and then I stopped myself. Why couldn't I turn off my radar? This wasn't even my business!

At that moment the door to the emergency room slid open once again. A tall blond woman dressed in a white pantsuit practically marched inside, straight over to Danielle.

"Danielle, why on earth did you bring Brad here?" the woman demanded in a Scandinavian-sounding accent. "We have perfectly good natural remedies at the retreat to help him."

"Sorry, Inge," she said, and dropped the forms on the desk. "I panicked when Brad almost passed out."

Bess and I were stunned when this Inge lady

walked over to Brad and pulled him out of the chair.

"My car is out front," Inge said, leaning Brad on Danielle's shoulder. "Let's go."

"Do you see that?" Bess asked as the three headed toward the door. "She's taking that poor guy out of the hospital."

I couldn't believe it.

"Excuse me," I called to Inge. "The doctor was just going to check him out."

Inge barely glanced at me before the door slid shut behind them. Seconds later Dr. Wainwright returned, looking for Brad.

"They just left," I said with a shrug. "With some blond woman."

"Left?" Dr. Wainwright said. "That's weird."

"That was weird," Bess agreed as I sat down. "Why were those two so scared of that woman?"

"I have no idea," I admitted. "But she did mention something about a retreat. She had some yellow emblem on her pocket, but I couldn't make out what it was."

"Wait a minute—a retreat?" Bess asked, her eyes wide. "What if that creepy Inge works next door to us at Roland's Renewal Retreat and Spa?"

"What are the odds of that, Bess?" I asked. "There must be more retreats and spas on Malachite Beach."

"I guess." Bess sighed. Her eyes suddenly lit up as

George entered the waiting room, a white bandage wrapped around her ankle.

"Dr. Viola found shards of glass in my cut," George said with a grin. "Which means I didn't step on the needle."

"That's great," Bess said, giving her cousin a big hug. I giggled as George grimaced. She was about as affectionate as a sumo wrestler in the ring.

I was just as relieved. But my questions still hadn't been answered. One: Did the needle really belong to the Casabian sisters? Two: What was it filled with? And three: Were there any more where that came from?

I knew I'd said we wouldn't try to find any mysteries while on vacation. But I had a funny feeling a mystery had just found us.

SPA SECRETS

"What are Dr. Viola's orders?" I asked George as we drove back to the house.

"I got a tetanus shot." George raised her arm to show a small Band-Aid. "I have to keep my foot dry for a day or two."

"There goes swimming and surfing," said Bess.

"We'll be in Malachite Beach for three weeks, Bess," George said. "At least I didn't step on that needle."

"That's for sure," Bess agreed. "Now the hospital can dispose of it safely. They deal with hundreds of needles every day."

"Actually," George said, "I asked Dr. Viola to send

the contents to the lab anyway. If the Casabian sisters were doing illegal drugs and trespassing, someone ought to know."

My hands froze on the steering wheel. As much as I thought the sisters had dumped trash on our beach, the last thing I wanted was to spread a rumor that they were users.

"George, you didn't tell that to Dr. Viola, did you?" I said. "Celebrity gossip spreads like wildfire around here."

"I'm not stupid, Nancy." George smirked. "I just told the doctor that if the needle had anything toxic in it, we would want to tell the police."

"Spoken like a true detective." Bess smiled.

"Speaking of the sisters, as soon as we get back, I want to go straight to Villa Fabuloso. I'm going to show them what they did to me," George said.

"Let it go, George," Bess pleaded. "Fighting with Mandy and Mallory would just be bad karma."

I could see George roll her eyes in the mirror.

In no time we were back at the house. While we made sandwiches for lunch, Bess and I told George about the drama in the waiting room.

"See what you missed?" I joked.

"I'm glad I did," George said as she twisted open a pickle jar. "I think I've had enough drama from one morning, which is why I'm *not* calling home. My parents would freak if they knew I'd been in a hospital ER."

After lunch I went out on the deck to call my dad. Even though he was Carson Drew, distinguished attorney and helper of all things mystery, I decided not to worry him, either, about the hypodermic needle on the beach.

"Guess what, Dad?" I asked. "We have celebrities living right next door."

"Celebs, huh?" I heard Dad's voice say. "Anybody I know?"

"The Casabian sisters," I said. "Ever hear of them?"

"Casabian sisters," Dad said slowly. "Weren't they a singing group in the eighties?"

"The eighties?" I laughed. "Oh, Dad, we have got to get you into the twenty-first century once and for all."

"Hey, no fair," Dad said. "I have an iPod."

"Because I gave you one for Father's Day," I reminded him. From the corner of my eye I could see Bess and George step out on the deck. "Dad, I'm going to go. We've got to figure out what to do on our first full day in L.A."

"I've got to go too," Dad said quickly. "Bye, sweetie."

"Bye, Dad." As I ended the call, I knew what to get him for next Father's Day—a cordless kitchen speakerphone.

"What's on the agenda?" George asked.

"Bess and I have to finish cleaning up the beach," I said.

"Then what?" Bess asked.

"My foot is still kind of sore," George said as she lowered herself into a chair. "So forget a lot of walking like Universal Studios or Rodeo Drive—thank goodness."

Bess's shoulders slumped. Then almost immediately she seemed to perk up.

"Why don't we go next door to Roland's Renewal Retreat and Spa?" she suggested. "We can get basic manicures, which would be a treat after picking up all that garbage."

I smiled at the thought. If anything could relax me, it was a luxurious manicure and hand massage.

"Sounds good," I said. "And lucky you, Bess, we might even meet Mia Casabian over there."

"What about you, George?" Bess asked.

George heaved a big sigh before saying, "Sure. Anything but Rodeo Drive."

After Bess called the spa to make appointments for manicures later that afternoon, she and I finished cleaning up the beach, this time wearing gloves, sneakers and thick socks. We found no more hypodermic needles but plenty of makeup containers with the yellow starburst design.

"Done!" Bess declared when our last trash bag was filled. "Now let's get these hardworking hands buffed and buttered."

Bess, George, and I walked along the road until we reached the pink stucco mansion at the end of the beach. Two men wearing "Roland's Renewal Retreat and Spa" T-shirts pulled open the massive gate to let us through. I noticed yellow emblems on their T-shirts—yellow sunburst emblems.

"You guys," I said as we made our way up the long driveway to the mansion, "did you see the logos on those shirts? I'm pretty sure they're the same as—"

"The makeup bottles we found on the beach." George nodded. "Yeah, I noticed it too."

"Most spas sell their own products," Bess said. "The Casabian sisters might buy their makeup here."

When we reached the front door of the mansion, George whistled through her teeth. "You'd think Brad and Angelina lived here," she said.

"They probably did at one time," I joked.

After stepping up to the heavy wood and iron door, George pulled a cord that rang the bell.

"Sounds like wind chimes," Bess pointed out.

"At least it's not some tacky TV tune like the Casabians'," George said.

It wasn't long before a young woman wearing a

black tunic and matching leggings pulled the door open. I noticed how perfect her hair and makeup were—lips glossy, eyelashes curled, bangs and layers thick and bouncy.

"I'm Luna," the woman chirped. "And you are?"

Bess introduced herself, then added, "And my friends are Nancy and George."

"George?" Luna said, raising a perfectly arched eyebrow. "Is that your real name?"

"No," George replied with a smirk. "It's Henry."

"George!" Bess hissed. She smiled at Luna and said, "Her real name is Georgia. But she hates her real name more than she hates—"

"Spas?" George cut in.

"Well, the name Georgia is lovely," Luna said. "Are you here for one of our treatments?"

"We each have an appointment for the basic manicure," Bess explained. "I made them about an hour ago."

"Then please come in." Luna made a sweeping motion with her hand to whisk us in. "I'll show you where to change into your robes and get a glass of fresh pomegranate juice."

"Robes?" George asked as we stepped through the door. "For a manicure?"

"Relax and enjoy," Bess said.

Following Luna, we crossed under a huge wrought-iron chandelier and down a long hallway. Candles flickered from iron sconces hanging from burgundy-colored walls. The air smelled like orange blossoms and cinnamon from the scented candles.

"Mmm," I said as I closed my eyes to take a whiff. Suddenly—

"Hot stuff coming through!" a voice barked.

My eyes snapped open. A guy with sandy-brown hair was coming down the hall. He was wearing faded jeans and a black T-shirt. He walked almost zombielike past us, holding a steaming mug of what smelled like peppermint tea.

"Cute . . . but snooty," Bess murmured. "He didn't even look at us."

I watched the guy as he continued down the hall. Where had I seen him before?

"Over here, ladies!" Luna stood outside a door farther down the hall. "Here's our waiting room."

Waiting room? I thought.

WAITING ROOM!

So that's who the zombielike guy was!

BEHIND CLOSED DOORS

"**B**ess," I said. "That's Brad from the emergency room at Malachite General."

"I think you're right," she whispered.

Vacation or not, I had to find out what was up with Brad.

"Nancy, where are you going?" Bess called as I raced the other way down the hall.

"Excuse me," I said when I caught up with Brad.

Brad turned around. He cocked his head as if to say, *Do I know you?*

"I'm Nancy," I said with a smile. "I just wanted to see how you were feeling."

"Feeling?" Brad asked, stone-faced.

"I saw you in the hospital earlier with Danielle," I explained. "You looked pretty sick. Actually, you're still pretty pale—"

"I'm fine," Brad interrupted, making me blink. "I just had . . . too much sun."

Then he slipped into a room off the hallway.

If he had too much sun, I thought, *why is he so pale?*

As I made my way back to the waiting room, I felt the color drain from my own face. If Brad was at this retreat, then that scary Inge probably was too.

"Well, it's about time," George said when I joined them. What a waiting room: low lights, soft music, and water cascading gently down one wall.

Luna handed me a white terry-cloth robe and matching slippers. "You and your friends can change behind any of the screens," she said, and then left us alone.

We talked to one another over the partitions as we changed into our robes.

"So was that guy Brad?" George asked.

"Not only was he Brad," I said, "he seemed annoyed when I asked him how he felt. He said he was much better, even though he still looked pretty sick."

"He *was* walking kind of like a zombie," Bess remembered.

"He spoke like one too," I said. "Which makes the whole thing even weirder."

The three of us stepped out from behind the screens at practically the same moment. The sight of us in those plushy white robes and slippers made me smile.

"Nancy, I just thought of something," Bess said. "If Brad is here, I bet crazy-lady Inge is too."

"I thought that too, Bess. But we don't know why she wanted Brad to leave the hospital," I said.

"Maybe Brad got sick from a spa treatment and they want to cover it up," Bess gasped.

"I think we should look for Inge and ask her some questions," I said.

"No way!" George was furious. "Nancy, didn't you say we should take a break from mysteries while on vacation? You don't even know who these people are!"

"But how can we not get involved after what happened to you on the beach?" Bess asked.

"*You* said we need to come here to relax," George said. "So let's just relax!"

Bess and I looked at each other. George was right. Taking a deep breath, I poured myself a glass of pomegranate juice, secretly hoping it wouldn't make me sick.

We sat quietly, sipping juice and listening to the gentle gurgling of the waterfall. As amped up as I was, the room did have a relaxing effect on me.

"Ladies?" Luna said softly as she stepped into the room. "Your hand specialists are ready for you now."

"Hand specialists?" George asked. "Are you sure we're getting manicures?"

We followed Luna into the hall. She opened a door and held it as we filed through. Three women dressed in white suits with the yellow starburst logo stood behind neatly arranged manicure tables.

"Come right in," one said cheerily.

"You bet." I smiled as I walked to a table.

Here I was in Malachite Beach, about to get a pampering spa treatment. Life was good, even if it was a little crazy sometimes.

After we were seated, the manicurists introduced themselves: Lotus, Ivy, and Cinnamon. NO kidding.

Ivy studied George's nails and asked, "When was the last time you had a manicure?"

Bess and I traded looks that said, *Uh-oh*.

"The last time," George said slowly. "Let's see . . . it was . . . about . . . never."

"No problem," Ivy said perkily. "We're not here to judge at Roland's Renewal Retreat and Spa."

Lotus gently placed my fingertips in two bowls filled with soothing warm water. "Ivy is right," she said. "This retreat is not only about outer beauty but inner beauty as well."

"I never saw myself on the inside," George said.

I felt the stress of the last two days slowly melt away. Instead of focusing on dirty hypodermic needles, drama queen sisters, and crazy ladies in white suits, I focused on the scent of the rose water. Leave it to Bess to ask, "Is there a woman named Inge working at this spa? A tall blond woman with a European accent?"

"Oh, I'm so sorry," Cinnamon said. "But we can't talk about other employees."

But Bess wouldn't give up. "Do you know Mia? Mia Casabian? I heard she's a guest here."

"We can't talk about the guests, either. But we *can* tell you everything we know about the retreat," Lotus said.

"Okay," I said while Lotus dried my hands with a fluffy white towel. "I'd like to know why they call it a retreat as well as a spa."

Lotus smiled and said, "Roland's Renewal Retreat and Spa is a place for people to retreat from everyday stress and life's challenges."

"Who is this guy Roland?" George asked while Ivy worked hard at digging dirt from under her nails. "Or are we not allowed to talk about him, either?"

The manicurists beamed on hearing Roland's name.

"Oh, yes!" Lotus exclaimed. "We're happy to talk about Roland."

"Roland is not only the owner of the spa, he's an incredible teacher," Ivy said.

"What does he teach?" Bess asked.

"Roland teaches his students how to connect with the light that shines from within us," Cinnamon said.

"And to cleanse the mind of negative, harmful thoughts," Lotus went on.

So . . . Roland was a kind of New Age motivational speaker. There was nothing wrong with teaching people to think positively. The question was, how did someone like Inge or that zombie Brad fit into this philosophy?

"Oh, dear," Ivy said, interrupting my thoughts. She was leaning over to look at George's bandaged ankle. "What happened to you?"

"I stepped on a piece of glass," George replied.

"There was trash all over our beach this morning," Bess explained.

"We're not totally sure where it came from," I said as Lotus massaged my hands. "We just have a theory."

The manicurists smile. They seemed to share a lot of little secrets.

"We know where the trash came from," Cinnamon said.

"You do?" Bess asked, practically rising from her chair. "Where?"

George and I leaned forward. Did the manicurists know things about the Casabian sisters?

"Well," Ivy said as she began filing George's nails, "chances are you willed that trash on the beach."

"Willed?" Bess, George, and I chorused.

"Through what Roland calls 'garbage thinking,'" Ivy said a little too excitedly.

"Garbage in," Cinnamon said with a little shrug, "garbage out."

The three of us slumped back in our chairs. Back to square one.

"Silly us," George said sarcastically. "Next time we'll think of bunny rabbits and unicorns."

"It's all in Roland's book, *You Are That*," Lotus went on. "It's attracted many followers—I mean fans."

"Can we meet Roland?" I asked.

"What for?" George mouthed to me.

Lotus shook her head and said, "Sorry. Only those who check into the retreat for intense renewal get to meet Roland."

"But you can look at his portrait," Cinnamon said. She nodded her chin at a gold-framed portrait hanging on the wall. It showed a towheaded guy sitting in a red velvet chair, surrounded by flowers. His hands were gently folded in his lap as he smiled serenely.

54

"Long live the king," George said.

Roland's portrait did look pretty regal for a guy who owned a spa. But the way the manicurists gazed at his portrait told me he was a lot more than that.

"Roland lets us do his fingernails and toenails sometimes," Cinnamon said. "If we're lucky."

Ivy jumped to her feet and wheeled over a cart filled with nail polish bottles.

"Go ahead and choose your colors," she said, sweeping her hand over the cart. "May I suggest choosing a shade to match your aura?"

"How about one to match my keyboard?" George laughed, grabbing a bottle of grayish-beige polish off the cart.

Bess finally picked a funky aquamarine shade, and I went with a cool coral. We were at a beach, after all.

We totally relaxed while Lotus, Ivy, and Cinnamon worked their magic on our hands. By the time we said good-bye and left, even George was admiring her nails.

"I think I can get used to manicures," she admitted. "At least once every few years."

We returned to the waiting room to change back into our regular clothes.

"This spa definitely does good work," Bess said, pulling on her sandals. "But you have to admit that whole Roland thing sounds bizarre."

"What's bizarre is how the manicurists weren't

allowed to talk about Inge—or anyone else," I pointed out. "Not even tell us if she works here."

"It's like Roland is some kind of rock star," George said.

"More than that," I said. "It sounds like he has some kind of power or influence over everyone here."

By now I was really curious about the retreat. Maybe we could talk some more to Brad or even find Mia. I glanced at the clock over the juice cart and said, "We don't have to leave yet. Why don't we check the place out before we go?"

"Sure," George finally agreed. "I'm kind of curious now too."

When we asked Luna for a tour of the retreat, she shook her head. "The retreat is in the west wing," she said. "Only those who sign up for the intense renewal get a tour."

"Oh," I said, disappointed.

"But I'll be happy to sign you up for more treatments," Luna added perkily.

Great, I thought. How were we going to see the retreat now?

"Um," George blurted. "I think I forgot something in the waiting room. Come on, Nancy, Bess. Help me find it."

"Okay," I said, knowing that George never forgot a thing.

We left Luna in the foyer. But instead of heading to the waiting room, we continued down the hall. We passed more treatment rooms, some marked WAXING, MASSAGE, and EYEBROW THREADING.

"This is still the spa part," Bess whispered. "I wonder where the west wing Luna was talking about is?"

"The ocean in California is west," I said. "I would think the west wing is on the beach side of the mansion."

"Which would be toward the back," George said, pointing ahead. "Forward march."

We walked farther and reached a set of double doors, which led to another hallway. Along this hall were closed doors, and at the end, a spiral staircase.

"Let's see where that leads," I said.

Quietly we climbed the stairs to a large, open room.

"Wow," George said.

Wow was right. The room was dark, with only a small lamp giving light. Scattered all over the floor were colorful pillows, large enough to be used as seat cushions. At the back of the room was a small stage, and on it was the red velvet chair from Roland's portrait.

"This is probably where Roland speaks," I said, keeping my voice low.

Then I heard voices that seemed to be coming

from behind a door near the stage. Walking closer, I saw a door with a small brass sign nailed to it.

"'Therapeutic Healing Room,'" I read aloud.

"Healing for what?" George whispered.

The voices grew louder as people began to shout: "You're fat!" "You're pathetic!" "You're a loser!" "Loser, loser, loser!"

Fat? Pathetic? Loser? I couldn't believe my ears. What was therapeutic about *insults*?

WAVES AND WARNINGS

"That's not healing," I said with a frown. "It's verbal abuse."

We were pressing our ears against the door, when a frosty voice made us jump.

"May I help you?"

Bess, George, and I whirled around. A tall woman with blond hair loomed over us.

Omigod! Inge!

"What are you doing here?" Inge asked.

I stared at the emblem on Inge's jacket, close enough to see that it was the retreat's yellow starburst logo.

"We just had manicures," Bess replied. She wiggled

her freshly polished fingers in front of her. "We wanted to know what else the spa offers."

Inge nodded at the closed door. "I'm afraid this is not part of the spa package, ladies," she said.

"Yeah, we figured that," said George.

"May I see you out?" Inge asked.

I stared up at Inge, who was about three inches taller than me. "We know the way, thanks," I replied.

Inge remained by the closed door as we hurried down the spiral staircase and out of the west wing. Luna was nowhere in sight after we paid for our manicures and headed back to Stacey's.

"That place may give good manicures," Bess shivered. "But it also gives me the creeps."

"Me too," I said. "All that yelling upstairs must be part of the 'intense renewal.'"

"A whole week of being called a pathetic loser?" George cried.

"Maybe renewal means different things to different people," Bess suggested.

"I suppose," I said. "But do you think that's what Mia Casabian is a part of?"

"Stop worrying," George said. "If Mia's the sensible sister, I'm sure she's fine."

George had a point. What we'd heard behind that door was definitely disturbing, but we'd never actually seen what was going on.

"Maybe you're right," I said. "Okay, you two, let's forget about the last two days and get back to some serious vacay."

"Why don't we change into our suits and head down to the beach? It's too late to sightsee anyway," George said.

"But Dr. Viola said no swimming for the next day or two," I reminded her.

"Who needs swimming?" George said as we approached the house. "I've got my laptop with me."

It didn't take long for us to change. The beach was clean again, but we spread our towels in a totally different spot, just to be safe.

As I lay down on my towel, I realized how tired I was from such a frenzied morning. And after a long winter, the sun on my face felt awesome.

George opened her laptop and searched for things to do in L.A. "How about the La Brea Tar Pits?" she asked. "They have giant prehistoric mammals covered in tar."

"Mm-hmm," I replied, too relaxed to answer. I could feel myself drifting off to sleep when—

"Yo!" a voice shouted. "Dudes!"

"Huh?" I said, my eyes snapping open.

Two guys were walking along the shore, carrying surfboards. "It's the Casabian sisters' boyfriends," I whispered.

Bess shaded her eyes with her hand. "It *is* Ty and Devon," she said excitedly.

"They're on our beach again," George said, annoyed. "Did they come back to dump more trash?"

"Hey," Ty said. "Mind if we say hi?"

"You just did," I replied.

Devon lifted his shades to gaze beyond us toward the shed. "Whoa. My little eye spies three excellent surfboards over there."

"They belong to Stacey," George said. "You know, the person who also owns this beach?"

"She left them for us," Bess explained.

"Excellent!" Ty exclaimed. "Then why don't you each grab a board and rock the breakers with us?"

"Rock the breakers?" I repeated.

"Surf the waves," Bess translated. She turned back to Ty and Devon. "Sorry, but George was the one who really wanted to surf, and she can't get her foot wet. She stepped on—"

"Trash," George finished. "You know, the kind you dumped last night?"

Ty and Devon looked sincerely confused.

"We don't know what you're talking about," Ty said. "But if you can't surf, I hear you."

"Just thought we'd ask," Devon added, shrugging.

I watched as the boys picked up their boards and turned toward the ocean.

"As if they didn't know about the trash," George said. "Give me a break."

I just couldn't help myself. "But if they did, we'll *never* find out," I said. "They're leaving before we can ask them anything."

"Not necessarily." Bess smiled slyly. She stood up and walked toward the guys. "Hey, guys? Where are you going?"

The boys turned around and smiled.

"So . . . what's up?" Ty asked Bess.

"Maybe George can't go in the water," Bess said cheerily. "That doesn't mean Nancy and I can't be schooled in surfing."

"Cool beans!" Ty said.

"Grab your boards and let's rock," Devon said.

"Okay," Bess agreed.

"Do you think Mandy and Mallory will want to surf with us?" I asked. Not that I wanted the Casabian sisters to join us. Mandy had already denied dumping the trash.

"Nah," Ty flapped his hand. "Mandy and Mallory are taping that show like they do all the time."

Bess and I passed George on our way to the shed. She glanced up and said, "Good luck."

Although I already knew how to surf a little, the Pacific was way bigger than anything I had ever seen. So we took it slow. We paddled our boards out in the water, where we tried several times to "pop up"—or jump up from a reclining position.

Bess and I did more wiping out than popping up. But eventually she managed to stand on her board and ride a wave for about thirty seconds. A big deal, according to Ty and Devon.

As for me, I was able to stand briefly, but kept wiping out and falling into the water. I had a blast, and almost forgot the real reason Bess and I had wanted to surf with Devon and Ty in the first place.

After the guys showed off some moves such as top turns and aerials, Bess and I got down to business. So much for promises.

"So how do you guys have such massive energy?" I asked while we paddled peacefully on our surfboards. "I mean, you were all on the beach so incredibly late last night."

"Us?" Ty asked. He shook his head. "We left before Mandy and Mallory did."

"The producer, Bev, wanted shots of just the girls," Devon explained. "No reason for Ty and me to hang out."

"Oh," I said, feeling the waves roll gently beneath my board. "So you all went clubbing *after* they finished shooting."

"Clubbing?" Ty repeated as his hand splashed in the water. "We didn't do any clubbing last night."

"Hey!" Devon said, practically sitting up on his board. "Did Mandy and Mallory go without us?"

Uh-oh. Opening a can of worms was not what I had in mind.

"No, no," I lied quickly. "I mean, I don't know if they went clubbing or not. . . ."

"We just thought all A-list celebs went out every night in Hollywood," Bess said. "I mean, don't they?"

The guys smiled at Bess. They then offered to teach us more new moves.

"We really have to get back to George," Bess said.

"Thanks anyway," I added.

"How about tomorrow morning?" Devon asked. "Ten o'clock?"

Bess and I exchanged shrugs. We had gotten all the information we needed out of the guys. But not all the surfing lessons.

"Maybe," I said.

"See ya," Bess called back as we paddled to shore.

Once on the beach, Bess and I placed our boards next to George.

"So how did it go?" she asked.

"I carved my first wave!" Bess said happily.

"Not the surfing, the questioning," George said. "Did they admit it?"

"On the contrary," I said as Bess and I sat on our

towels. "They left the beach *before* the sisters did. They were clueless about the trash."

"So the sisters could have wrecked the beach on their own," Bess added.

"Let's just hope it doesn't happen again," I said.

The three of us spent another half hour on the beach before we collected our stuff and surfboards and headed back to the house.

Once inside, we saw the message light blinking on Stacey's phone.

"Looks like Stacey got a call," George said.

"How do we know it's not for us?" asked Bess.

"Did you give her number to anyone? Everyone at home knows we have our cells," George replied.

"We'd better answer it," I said, grabbing a pad and pen. "It could be an important message for Stacey."

I walked over to the phone and pressed the play button. After a few seconds of dead air, a mechanical-sounding voice began to speak:

"If you know what's good for you, girls, you'll never, EVER, mess with us again."

Click.

8

MYSTERY CRUISE

"That *was* for us," I said slowly.

"Unfortunately," Bess added.

"I'm calling Stacey," George said. "Or the police. This is getting dangerous."

"Wait," I said.

I played the message once, twice, listening for any sign as to who'd left it. But the robotic-sounding voice offered no clues.

"Why does the voice sound so mechanical?" Bess asked.

"Some phones have electronic voice changers on them," George explained. "You press a button and the voice is disguised to sound just like that one."

Again I played the message, writing down every word. "The caller said not to mess with 'us,'" I pointed out.

"Us as in more than one," George said, narrowing her eyes. "The sisters."

"But why would Mandy and Mallory threaten us?" Bess wanted to know. "*We're* the ones who should be mad that they messed up our beach."

"Those spoiled brats are probably not used to being told off," George said.

"Do you still want to call Stacey, George?" Bess asked. "Or the police?"

George stared at the phone, then shook her head. "If it is those ditzy sisters, we can handle them," she said. "I don't want to disturb Stacey unless it's totally necessary."

"I'm pretty sure the message was left by Mandy and Mallory too," I agreed. "But until we have more proof, we can't be absolutely sure."

"Just like the needle, huh?" George said, glancing down at her wrapped ankle.

"What if Mandy and Mallory *are* out to get us?" Bess asked slowly. "I mean, what if their show is going in a whole new sinister direction?"

"Sinister direction?" I asked.

"You know." Bess shrugged. "From *Chillin' with the Casabians* to *Killin' with the Casabians*?"

"Come on, Bess, that's ridiculous," I said, but didn't delete the message, in case we did decide to go to the police.

"So, where should we go tonight? My foot is feeling much better," George asked.

As Bess opened her mouth to speak, George added, "Other than Rodeo Drive."

"For your information, I was going to suggest Santa Monica Pier," Bess answered. "We can grab dinner and go to that amusement park on the pier. I think it's called Pacific Park."

"Sounds neat," I said.

"Yeah," George said. "There are some wild rides there."

I smiled at the thought of wild rides. So far Malachite Beach had been one wild ride for us—and it was only our second day.

We found the perfect place to eat, with an incredible view of the ocean. We stuffed ourselves with crispy coconut shrimp, root beer, and hush puppies and then strolled through the amusement park.

Colorful lights from the rides glowed brightly against the purple-gray sky. Carnival-style music filled the warm, salty air. So did the smell of cotton candy and roasted peanuts.

"I did a search on Pacific Park before we left the house," George said, pointing to an illuminated Ferris wheel in the distance. "That ride over there is solar powered."

"Even the rides in L.A. are green," I said. "How cool is that?"

Bess turned away from the rides. She nodded at the coin-operated telescopes along the long part of the pier. "Let's try out one of those before the rides," she suggested.

"What are you looking for?" I asked. "Exotic California seabirds?"

"Exotic California celebrities." Bess smiled as she slipped a quarter into the telescope. "From here you can see a long stretch of Malachite Beach. Maybe I'll see private beaches and celebrity mansions all lit up."

"Spy," George accused.

"I prefer the word voyeur, thank you," Bess said as she adjusted the telescope and peered through.

A gull landed on the rail a few inches away from me. After checking us out, it flapped its wings and took off.

"What do you see?" I asked Bess.

"Oh, wow," she said, her eyes pressed against the telescope. "There's our beach and Villa Fabuloso. And I can see the beach behind Roland's Renewal Retreat and Spa. The one right next to ours."

"We came all the way to Santa Monica to look at our own beach?" George complained. "Let's just go on the rides."

"No, really!" Bess said. She tilted the telescope to the left ever so slightly. "There are three small row-boats heading in the direction of the yacht. The big one we saw the other day."

"You mean the yacht anchored off the retreat?" I said. "Maybe the guests are going on some moon-light meditation cruise."

"Or moonlight *confrontation* cruise," George said.

I frowned as I remembered the screaming and yell-ing behind the closed door, and Brad in the emer-gency room. Could he be in one of the boats?

"Hasn't your quarter run out yet, Bess?" George asked.

Bess was leaning forward, peering through the telescope. "Now people are stepping out of the small boats onto the yacht. Omigod! One of them looks like Mia!"

"Mia Casabian?" I asked. I tried to see the yacht and the people, but without a telescope, all the boats were just specks. "Let me look, Bess."

Bess stepped aside. "Mia has shoulder-length dark hair. She's wearing jeans and a red-and-white-striped T-shirt," she said.

I found her immediately.

"I wonder if Mia signed up for that weeklong intensive," I said. "The one the manicurists were tell-ing us about."

"According to Mandy and Mallory, she's been there longer than a week," George said.

"Why doesn't she want to go home?" I said, still watching Mia as she stepped aboard the yacht. "Maybe that reality show got to her. Or maybe she was sick of being the 'plain' sister."

"Or maybe she was just sick of her sisters!" George said. "My turn to look through that thing."

I stepped aside. But the moment George peered through—

"The quarter ran out!" she groaned.

"I didn't see anyone famous except for Mia," Bess complained. She held out her hand. "Anyone have another quarter?"

I was wondering about Mia, but not enough to spend our first night out spying through a telescope.

"Enough stargazing," I said. "Let's check out that Ferris wheel."

"It's eighty-five feet high," George said once we were seated inside our dangling car.

"TMI!" Bess groaned.

Once on the Ferris wheel, it was a slow but breathtaking ride to the top. Even Bess agreed the view was awesome.

"Who needs a telescope?" she exclaimed. "You can see all of L.A. from up here."

As I glanced in the direction of the yacht, my thoughts drifted back to Mia.

What's going on in that retreat? I wondered. *And why won't Mia Casabian come home?*

"Watch out, Pacific," George exclaimed. "Here I come!"

It was the next morning, and the three of us were carrying surfboards to the beach. Instead of the gauzy white bandage from yesterday, George was wearing a lighter adhesive one.

"Dr. Viola said it would be okay to go swimming today," she said. "I just hope Ty and Devon don't mind another surfer."

"At least there was no garbage on the beach when we woke up," I said.

"Just an innocent casualty," Bess said.

"Huh?" George asked.

We looked to see where Bess was pointing. There, lying stiffly on the sand, was a seagull. An undoubtedly dead seagull.

"I bet it got something stuck in its throat," Bess said.

"Great." I sighed. "We must have missed some trash when we were cleaning up yesterday."

"There is something you missed," George said. She pointed to the back of my surfboard.

I flipped my board around and froze. Bright orange letters were scrawled across it:

GO BACK TO RIVER HIGHTS BEFORE IT'S TOO LATE!

9

SISTERLY SUSPECTS

"Whoever wrote it," I said, "spelled River Heights wrong."

"What do you mean, *whoever* wrote it?" George exclaimed. "Who else? The Casabians."

We checked the other two boards for more messages. Nothing—but that threat was enough to creep me out.

"It had to be Mandy and Mallory," Bess said, tilting her head to study the message. "They used lipstick. Tangy Tangerine, Mallory's favorite shade."

I could see George taking deep breaths to keep from losing it. But she wasn't the only one who was angry about what had happened.

"We're going to their house right now," George ordered. "We're not leaving until Mandy and Mallory own up to what they've done."

I nodded. "They can't get away with trashing beaches and threatening people."

"What about our surfing lesson?" Bess asked. She pointed to Ty and Devon riding the waves. "The guys are probably waiting for us."

I shook my head as I watched Ty and Devon carve the same wave. "Are those two really that clueless about what's happening on our beach?" I asked.

"Woo-hoo," Ty cheered to Devon. "The waves today are, like, totally sick!"

"X-treme, dude, x-treme!" Devon shouted back.

George rolled her eyes. "They're clueless. Now let's pay their girlfriends a visit."

We returned our surfboards to the shed and walked to the villa. This time the door was opened, not by the housekeeper, but by Bev, the producer.

"Okay, here's the scene," Bev babbled to us. "You all come through the door and demand to see Mandy and Mallory."

"We were just going to do that," I said.

"Good," Bev snapped. She then turned and yelled over her shoulder. "We're taping here!"

Before I could say another word, we were blinded by the lights.

"I don't care if we're on TV or not," George said as she pushed her way inside. "It's time the world saw what those sisters are really about."

Bess and I followed George into the house. Unfortunately, the cameraman and soundman followed us. So did Mandy's dog Peanut Butter, yapping at our heels.

With Bev's help, we found Mandy and Mallory lounging on a snowy white sofa that swept halfway around the living room.

"I suppose you got our messages," Mandy said coolly.

"Your messages, huh?" George demanded. "So that voice mail and those lipsticky warnings *were* yours."

"By the way," Bess told the sisters, "River Heights is spelled with an *e*."

The camera was rolling, but I no longer cared. I stepped right up to them and said, "I know you two are famous, but what gives you the right to do what you did?"

Mandy jutted her chin out and said, "What gives *you* the right to steal our boyfriends?"

The three of us stared at the Casabians.

"Huh?" George asked.

Mallory began to sob. "We saw you surfing with Ty and Devon. And flirting with them too."

"Especially that redhead over there," Mandy said,

pointing at me. "Falling off her surfboard so Ty could help her."

"We were not flirting with them!" I insisted. "Okay, maybe Bess was—but it was only to get information."

"What information?" Mallory sniffed.

"On the mess that was made of our beach," I explained. "We thought the guys might know something about it."

From the corner of my eye, I could see the director motioning the camera and boom mike closer to me.

"You still think *we* did it?" Mandy demanded. "Seriously, do these look like hands that would have anything to do with garbage?"

To prove their point, Mandy and Mallory held out perfectly manicured hands.

"What about the messages?" I demanded.

"You had to have been trespassing to write on Nancy's surfboard," George said.

Peanut yipped as he jumped on Mallory's lap. Stroking the dog's silky fur, she said, "We called in the first message. That was easy."

"The other message was harder," Mandy said. "We had to wait until you left the house last night. That's when we snuck onto your beach and wrote the message on the board."

"So you *were* trespassing!" George said.

"Only for a few minutes," Mandy said. "Then we went to an awesome movie premiere in Westwood. But now that we know you're not after our guys, we won't be doing stuff like that anymore."

"Gee, thanks," George said sarcastically. "You're just lucky we didn't go to the police or call Stacey."

"That would have been awkward," Mallory said.

I was glad we got Mandy and Mallory to come clean about the messages. But there were still unanswered questions about the trash and that horrific needle.

"Can I ask you something?" I said. "Do you guys use makeup from Roland's Renewal Retreat and Spa? The package has a yellow sunburst design—"

"Never!" Mandy cut in.

The sisters then looked straight into the camera.

"We use only Foxy Girl products," Mallory said.

"Because in order to be foxy," Mandy said, a provocative gleam in her eye, "you have to *look* foxy!"

"And—cut!" Bev shouted. "Great way to plug our sponsors, girls."

Bess, George, and I exchanged looks.

That answered that.

Bev waved the cameraman over to Mallory on the sofa. "Let's get a one-shot," she said.

Peanut growled as Mallory tossed him off her lap. "What do I say?" she asked Bev.

"Talk about how relieved you are that the girls weren't stealing your boyfriends," Bev said quickly. "Blah, blah, blah."

Out of nowhere a woman rushed over to Mallory. She brushed powder over her face, then hurried out of the shot.

"Three, two, and one," Bev counted down before pointing to Mallory.

Bess, George, and I stood stunned as Mallory spoke directly to the camera. "We found out that the girls next door were not stealing our boyfriends. So, like, we left that message on their phone for nothing. I ruined my favorite lipstick for nothing too, which is totally stressing me out."

"Cut!" Bev shouted. "Let's take a ten-minute break, then shoot cutaways."

"We'll take a half hour." Mandy smiled at us. "Let's have coffee outside."

We left the crew inside to lounge on the Casabian sisters' deck. The five of us drank coffee and had our first real friendly chat.

"How do you like L.A.?" Mandy asked us.

"We love L.A.!" Bess answered, shooting George a look. "And when I finally see Rodeo Drive, I'll love it even more."

"We can take you there one day," Mandy said.

"Really?" I asked.

"Sure," Mallory said. "Let's all go out one night. We know the best clubs and places to eat—"

"And a lot of cute guys to introduce you to," Mandy added. "Unless you already have boyfriends."

"I do," I replied. "His name is Ned."

The sisters smiled when I showed them Ned's picture on my phone.

"Nice!" Mallory said.

I thought this was a good time to mention Mia. I still hadn't forgotten seeing her on the yacht last night.

"You two have boyfriends," I said slowly. "But what about Mia? Is she seeing anybody?"

Their faces dropped.

"Who knows *anything* about Mia these days?" Mallory said softly. "She's still over at that dumb spa."

"Well, we think we saw Mia last night. She was getting on a yacht with a bunch of other people," Bess said.

"You saw Mia?" Mandy gasped. She turned to Mallory and said, "She was probably on Roland's yacht."

"So it *is* Roland's yacht," I said.

Mallory nodded. "Everyone in Malachite keeps their yachts at the marina," she said. "Except Roland. He keeps his anchored off his beach at all times."

I wondered why that was, but I still had a few

more questions about Mia. "Why don't you go to the retreat and find out about your sister?"

"We've tried," Mandy said. "The first time we went, Mia told us she was fine. The next visit, some blond woman in a white suit told us that Mia didn't want to see us."

Blond woman in a white suit? Inge!

"Did you ever try calling or texting her?" George asked.

"Sure, but Mia doesn't answer," Mandy said.

"Except that one time," Mallory reminded her sister. "I got her to stay on for a few minutes, but it was weird. She sounded like a different person."

"A different person?" I repeated.

"Her voice was flat, and she kept going on and on about Roland," Mallory explained.

"Well, it gets even weirder," Mandy went on. "We just got a call from the bank asking about a huge withdrawal from Mia's account. I'm pretty sure Mia took out the money, but why would she need all that money in a place like that?"

"It's a mystery," Mallory said.

The word "mystery" made Bess, George, and me trade glances. Should we tell the sisters we were detectives?

Probably not.

Bev called Mandy and Mallory back into the house.

"Thanks for the coffee," George said. "But no more messages on Stacey's phone, okay?"

Mallory quickly looked over her shoulder, then whispered to us, "Those mean messages were Bev's idea."

"She said it would make great TV," Mandy added with a shrug. "Sorry."

"Apology accepted," I said. "Keep us posted on Mia, okay?"

"Deal," Mallory agreed.

On our way back to the house, we stopped on the beach, hoping the dead gull we had seen was a bad dream, but it wasn't—it was still there.

"I believe Mandy and Mallory when they said they didn't trash our beach," I admitted. "They seemed to have pretty solid alibis."

"How do we know they're solid?" George asked.

"I know a way we can find out," Bess said. She pulled out her phone and went online. "There's a site called Star Track. It tells you where and when celebrities are on the town—with tons of pictures."

"I'm supposed to be the computer geek here," George complained. "How come I didn't know about Star Track?"

"Because you're not star*struck*," I said with a smile. "Like Bess is."

George and I peered over Bess's shoulder. Music blared as a flashy home page appeared. Pictures of celebrities smiled out of blinking silver stars. One star contained a picture of the Casabian sisters.

"Perfect!" Bess said, clicking on the star.

Up popped photos of Mandy and Mallory. One showed them standing side by side on a red carpet dressed in animal print minidresses. Mandy's was zebra, Mallory's leopard.

"'Mandy and Mallory Casabian looking wild at the premiere of *Love Safari*,'" I read the caption aloud.

"It says the date of the premiere was last night," Bess pointed out. "Just as they said."

"Okay, so they didn't lie about last night," George said. "But what about two nights ago, when the garbage was dumped?"

Bess scrolled down to the next picture. It showed the sisters walking into a club called Tic-Tock two nights ago. A giant clock over the door read two o'clock.

"That's when I heard the voices," I said. "If Mandy and Mallory were clubbing late that night, they couldn't have been on the beach."

"Which means the sisters are clean," Bess said. "So if Mandy and Mallory didn't make that mess—who did?"

I didn't have a clue, until I remembered the yellow sunburst logo on the makeup containers. The sisters didn't use the spa's makeup, so . . .

"Could the *spa* have dumped the trash?" I asked.

"Why would a spa of all places throw garbage on our beach?" George wondered. "Or on any beach, for that matter?"

I felt the warm foam of a wave roll over my foot. Which made me think . . . "Maybe the spa didn't dump it—maybe it came in with the tide," I said.

"The tide?" George furrowed her brow. "I'm not getting this, Nancy."

"The *yacht*, George. What if they dumped their garbage off the yacht, into the ocean?"

"Why would they do that?" Bess asked.

"Maybe they're too cheap to hire a private trash pickup service," I said. "Or maybe they're too lazy to recycle."

"Especially if they use hypodermic needles," George said, glancing down at her foot. "They'd have to dispose of them in a nonhazardous way."

"So to save time or money," Bess went on, "the spa secretly dumps their trash? Maybe 'garbage in, garbage out' really does mean something."

"Maybe," I said. But I wasn't entirely convinced; it still seemed kind of strange to me.

Then George reminded us, "Well, the hospital should have the results on the needle soon, and we'll know what the spa is using them for."

"It's *got* to be Botox," Bess said. "I mean, did you see that portrait of Roland? It's a wonder he can still blink—he looks so weird."

"What's weird," I said, "is how Mandy and Mallory described Mia, like she's a whole new person."

Bess pointed to the next beach. "Why don't we find out for ourselves?" she said. I turned to see Mia Casabian, alone on the beach, doing tai chi.

"I know it's private property, but let's go talk to her," I said. "It's a long shot, but maybe she'll tell *us* why she never went home."

We walked along the shore to the retreat's beachfront.

"Hi, Mia," I called as we walked over. "Nice to meet you. I'm Nancy and these are my friends Bess and George."

"Are you fans?" Mia frowned.

"Yes, I mean, no, I mean . . ." Bess was flustered. "We're living in Stacey Manning's house while she's away on business."

Mia glanced at the mansion behind us.

"You're not supposed to be here," she said in almost a whisper. "This is the retreat's private beach."

"I know. We just want you to know your sisters are worried about you," I said.

"Why won't you go home, Mia?" George asked. "The pedicures here can't be *that* good."

Mia shook her head. "I can't. Roland says I have to focus on myself and the renewal process, not on my sisters."

"But Mandy and Mallory care about you," I said.

"That's what they want you to think," Mia answered. A smile swept slowly across her face. "Nobody cares for me as much as Roland."

What was up with this guy Roland? Most of all, what was up with this retreat?

"What's the renewal process all about, Mia?" I probed. "What do you have to do?"

"It's amazing!" Mia exclaimed. "For a whole week, students of Roland go through different challenges, both physical and mental."

"What kind of challenges?" George asked.

"Only students of Roland get to find out," Mia said with an apologetic smile.

I was just going to ask about Inge when someone called Mia's name. A guy who looked to be in his early twenties walked toward us. The sunburst logo on the shirt pocket told me he was a spa employee— or a Roland devotee.

"Time for your aura evaluation, Mia," he said with a tight grin.

"Thank you, Scotty," Mia said.

Without a good-bye, she turned and headed back to the mansion. But Scotty stayed behind with us.

"Can I help you?" he asked.

I nodded toward our own beach. "We're your neighbors," I explained. "We just came over to say hi to—"

"This beach is the private property of Roland and the retreat. You're not welcome," Scotty interrupted. He turned and walked quickly back to the mansion.

"I would have asked him about the trash," I finally said. "But he seemed way too scary."

"So did Mia," Bess said. "Did you see the way her eyes lit up whenever she talked about Roland?"

I did. And that made me think we had more to worry about than just the trash on the beach.

"You guys," I said, "I don't think Roland is running a spa here."

"Then what is it?" Bess asked.

"I think . . ." I paused and turned my eyes on the mansion. "It's a cult."

CULT CRASHERS

"A cult?" Bess repeated. "As in ... brainwashing?"

"Think about it," I said as we walked along the shore to our own beach. "Everyone we met at the retreat talks about Roland like he was their brilliant leader."

"Mia and that guy Brad did seem pretty zombie-like," George agreed.

"And don't most cults persuade followers to hand over their worldly possessions?" I pointed out.

"Mia's bank account," George remembered. "Roland could have convinced Mia to withdraw a huge chunk of money to hand over to him."

But when I looked at Bess, she seemed unconvinced.

"I can't believe stuff like that is happening next door," she insisted. "The spa seems so classy and well run."

"The spa could be a front for the cult and the perfect way to attract more followers, Bess," I said.

"Now you're giving me the creeps." Bess frowned.

As we turned onto our beach I wondered about Mia. Why was she so over the moon about Roland? And what about Brad? *What* had made him so dehydrated—enough to end up in the hospital?

What I said next surprised even me.

"Bess, George," I said. "I'm going back to Roland's Renewal Retreat and Spa. I'm signing up for the full-week intensive."

"What?" George asked, surprised.

"You mean you're joining that cult?" Bess cried.

"I'm not joining anything," I insisted. "I want to find out the truth about what's *really* going on."

George rolled her eyes to the sky. "Great," she groaned. "We get a fabulous beach house for three weeks and you want to waste an entire week in that kooky place."

"You don't need a week to find out if and why they're dumping their trash in the ocean, do you?" Bess asked.

"It's not just about the trash anymore," I said. "I want to see if I can help Mia. She acted so spacey. And the shouting we heard at the retreat was awful."

"So you're really going to do this?" George asked me. "What happened to taking a vacation from mysteries?"

"How can we relax knowing what might be going on right next door?" I asked.

"Okay, Nancy, but you're not going to that place alone," Bess said. "George and I are going there with you."

"What?" George cried. "We can't all leave Stacey's house after she put us in charge."

"George, you stay here. Bess and I will investigate. We might need you to look stuff up on the computer for us."

"Until they turn you into Roland-worshipping zombies too," George said. "What if that Inge doesn't let you sign up? After seeing us snooping around, she might know you're up to something."

"Good point," I admitted. "But we'll worry about Inge when the time comes."

"Maybe we should tell Mandy and Mallory we're going over," Bess suggested. "They might want to know we're trying to help Mia."

I shook my head. "If their producer Bev finds out, she'll storm the place with the camera crew.

Let's wait before we say anything," I said.

"So . . . when are you guys leaving?" George asked slowly.

"I think Bess and I should pack and go over there as soon as possible," I explained.

While Bess and I got ready, George made us double-stuffed sky-high sandwiches, just in case the food at the retreat consisted of a daily diet of water-cress and twigs.

"Good luck, you two," George said as we finally left the house. "Make sure you stay connected."

"We will," I promised. "Make sure you don't leave your phone or your computer."

Bess laughed. "Does she ever?"

Carrying our duffel bags, we made our way down the road to Roland's Renewal Retreat and Spa. Luna seemed genuinely happy to see us when she opened the door.

"Why, hello there," she greeted us. "Here for more treatments?"

I nodded at the bag on my shoulder and said, "Actually, we're here to sign up for the weeklong intensive."

Luna blinked with surprise. "Oh, my," she said. "In that case, come with me, please."

Instead of taking us to the spa's waiting room, Luna led us down another hallway. Stopping at a door at the end, she knocked four times and waited.

After a few seconds a voice said, "Come in."

Bess and I traded glances. The frosty voice was clearly Inge's.

As Luna opened the door, I could see Inge sitting regally behind a large mahogany desk. She peered at us over the glasses resting on the tip of her nose.

"Thank you, Luna," Inge said. She gestured to two chairs in front of her desk.

I was surprised when Inge flashed a cheery smile and said, "Please sit down. I had a feeling you'd be back."

"You did?" Bess asked.

"Yes," Inge said, folding her hands on her desk. "There was something in your faces that told me you wanted to know more."

Was Inge onto us?

"Um," I said, smiling at the elaborate portrait of Roland behind her desk. "We actually want to learn everything about Roland's philosophy."

"His book *You are That* seems so . . . inspiring!" Bess chimed in.

"How many times did you read it?" Inge asked.

"H–how many times?" Bess stammered.

"Most people sign up for the intensive and come back a few days later to begin." Inge looked at our luggage. "You seem ready to check in right away."

"We're only in town for a short time," Bess blurted.

"So we need to start now," I added.

Inge nodded as she observed us silently. Then her smile returned suddenly, and she said, "And so you shall!"

"Shall what?" I asked.

"Join the intensive. But before you begin the renewal process, you must fill out these forms," she said, and handed us two clipboards. "Remember to sign your names at the bottom."

Inge stood up and walked over to a nearby file cabinet. She pretended to be busy rummaging through the files, but I could feel her radar on us.

Bess and I filled out the first few lines—name, address, telephone number. I had no problem giving that information—until I reached the fourth line.

"They want our bank information?" I whispered.

"No way," Bess whispered. "Why should we give them that?"

"Is there a problem?" Inge asked.

"Um . . . we were just wondering why you need our bank info," I said.

"For the fee," Inge said as though we should have known. "And for any minor expenses that might come up."

"What is the fee?" I asked.

Inge waved her hand as if it wasn't important. "Eight thousand dollars," she said.

"Eight thousand dollars?" Bess squeaked.

"For a week?" I asked.

"Meals included," Inge added.

"You know," I blurted, "I don't remember my bank account number." I rolled my eyes as if to say, *Duh*.

"Neither do I," Bess said. "Can we give it to you another time maybe?"

"Or can't we just be billed later?" I asked.

Inge stared at us. "Wait here," she finally said.

She marched over to another door in her office, rapped on it three times, and slipped inside.

As soon as the door shut, Bess and I jumped from our chairs. We raced to the door, pressed our ears against it, and listened.

"Roland, I have two girls being resistant," we heard Inge say.

"Roland is in there," Bess whispered.

"Resistant how?" a deeper voice said.

"They won't cough up their bank information," Inge said. "Should I tell them to leave?"

Silence. And then . . .

"No, Inge," Roland said. "Let's wait until they finish the entire process. They'll be so spaced out they won't even know they're giving us their bank account numbers—or all their money."

I turned my head to stare at Bess. So that's what this retreat was all about. *Money!*

"Thank you, Roland," Inge said.

Bess and I zipped back to our chairs just before Inge opened the door.

"No bank information needed for now, girls," she declared. "Just sign at the bottom and you'll be ready to be renewed, revitalized, and recharged."

"Cool," Bess said with a smile.

I smiled too as we signed the forms. I didn't know whether to be excited or scared. I think I was a little of both—excited to be starting this investigation, scared of what we were about to find out.

"Good!" Inge said. She took the clipboards and held out her hand. "Now if I may have your cell phones, please."

"Our phones?" Bess gulped.

I thought of George back at the house expecting our calls. "Why do you want our phones?" I asked, trying not to sound panicky.

"So you can become totally immersed in the renewal process," Inge said, still with her hand out.

My head spun with excuses for needing my phone. Like I had to check in on my elderly dad every day. Inge didn't have to know he was only in his forties. Or that I couldn't start my day without my daily horoscope alert.

Luckily, Bess had it already figured out.

"Here's my phone," she said, holding out her cell.

"Nancy doesn't have a phone. Yesterday she dropped it in the La Brea Tar Pits."

"I see," Inge said slowly.

That seemed to do it, but I secretly hoped my phone wouldn't go off in my pocket.

"Let's go, ladies," Inge said. "I'll take you to your room."

Bess and I followed Inge out of the office and up a flight of stairs to the living quarters.

"Home sweet home," Inge said, opening a door.

Bess and I stepped into a room with dark brown carpeting and peach-colored walls. Against the wall was a Spanish-style dresser but no mirror. There were two full-size beds with black iron headboards—but no bedding.

"Are we getting any pillows or sheets?" I asked.

Inge shook her head. "There is no time for sleep," she said. "Reading Roland's teachings and working on his assignments during the night is recommended."

No sleep? But I forced a smile and said, "Yes, of course, totally. Thanks, Inge."

"Why don't you freshen up and we will see you in the dining room, six o'clock sharp," Inge said, and then left the room.

Once Inge's footsteps had faded away, we shut the door and groaned.

"Thank goodness there's a bathroom," I said,

pointing to a small bathroom off the room. "I was afraid they discouraged toilets, too."

"You'd think they'd want us to be alert and well rested," Bess said. "So we'd take in everything this Roland guy has to say."

"Unless they'd rather we be dazed and vulnerable," I suggested. "So we *believe* everything Roland has to say."

My thoughts were interrupted by my phone vibrating inside my pocket.

"Hello?" I answered.

"Hello yourself," George replied. "Why are you whispering?"

"We're not allowed to have phones," I said. "So far this place is totally weird, and we just got here."

"Well, it's about to get weirder," George said.

"Wait!" Bess put her ear to the phone. "This way we can both hear."

"Go ahead, George," I urged.

"Dr. Viola called me with the results of the hypodermic needle analysis. It contained a drug called sodium pentothal," she said.

"What's that?" Bess asked.

"According to this pharmaceutical site I'm looking at," George said, "some people call it a 'truth serum.' The drug is effective at weakening a person's resolve and making them suggestible to persuasion. It's been used in interrogations."

"So I guess it wasn't Botox," Bess said.

"The dose in the needle wasn't toxic, according to the doctor," George said. "But it could have made a person listless and loopy."

I wondered if the other needles we'd found contained sodium pentothal. But mostly I wondered why the retreat would be using the drug. And on whom?

"Thanks, George. We'll check in later," I whispered. "I don't want my battery to run out."

I clicked off my phone. Bess and I then sat on one of the beds.

"Mia seemed loopy to me," Bess decided. "I'll bet she was injected with that drug. Sodium . . . whatever."

"Sodium pentothal," I said. "I wouldn't be surprised if all the guests here get it. So they can become Roland's sock puppets."

"Nancy, *we're* guests here now," Bess said, a tinge of panic in her voice. "How are we going to keep away from the needles?"

CHALLENGES

"I like macaroni and cheese," I said during dinner. "I like bread, too. But I wish there was some other food to eat, like veggies or salad."

"I guess Roland doesn't believe in low-carb diets," Bess said, grabbing a slice of white bread. "I guess the eight-thousand-dollar fee isn't going toward food, either."

"That's because it's going into Roland's pocket," I said, lowering my voice.

I took a sip of the only beverage on the table—a flat orange soda. Could the retreat be depriving its members of sleep *and* nutrition?

"The mac and cheese is Roland's favorite," a perky voice interrupted my thoughts. "He says you can never have too much comfort food."

A college-age girl with curly blond hair was smiling at us from the other end of the table.

"Does he?" I asked.

"I'm Daisy Matthews," the girl said. She nodded at a raven-haired guy sitting next to her, probably the same age. "This is my friend Terrence Olivez."

Terrence's mouth was full, so he smiled with his eyes.

"Nancy Drew," I introduced myself.

"Bess Marvin," Bess said with a little wave. "So . . . you two come here often?"

"No." Daisy smiled. "Terrence and I are total newbies. I actually took a leave from college to come here."

"You left school just to come here?" Bess asked, surprised.

"I decided I'd rather study Roland's philosophy than any other subject," Daisy explained.

"And you, Terrence?" I asked. "Did you also take a leave of absence?"

"Nope," Terrence said a bit shyly. "I start college next fall."

Daisy leaned forward and whispered as if Terrence wasn't even there. "Terrence was always bullied in high school. He's afraid the same thing will happen in college unless he boosts his self-esteem."

"You think Roland can help you with that?" I asked Terrence directly.

"I bet Roland can do anything!" Daisy answered for her friend. "I read his book *You Are That* three times."

"Cool," I said. But was really thinking, *Give me a break.*

Daisy and Terrence went back to eating. I was about to take another forkful of macaroni when I spotted two familiar faces at the next table.

"Bess, don't look now," I whispered. "But look who's sitting at the next table."

"Nancy," Bess complained. "How can I not look and look at the same time—"

"It's Brad and Danielle," I told her. "From the ER at Malachite General."

We watched as Brad nibbled on a roll. Danielle seemed to have an appetite for her meal.

"Brad doesn't look so pale anymore," I whispered. "Danielle is less nervous too—probably because Inge's not around."

Our view was suddenly blocked as a middle-aged couple sat with us. They smiled at Bess and me as they placed their trays on the table.

"Are these seats taken?" the man asked with a friendly gleam in his eye.

"Yes, by you," Bess said, smiling.

The couple introduced themselves as Ralph and Linda Meyers. They were married, retired, and huge fans of Roland.

"We may be in our late sixties," Ralph said, "but it's never too late to be renewed."

"I'll drink to that!" Linda laughed, raising her glass of cola.

Bess and I excused ourselves from the table to get some coffee.

"No wonder everyone here walks around like zombies," Bess said after taking a sip of the watered-down coffee. "They're caffeine deprived."

"Or nutrition deprived," I said. "Unless keeping us weak and light-headed is part of Roland's plan."

We were about to carry our cups to our table when I felt someone tap my shoulder. Turning, I saw Mia, her mouth a thin, grim line.

"Hi, Mia," I said with a smile.

"I know why you two are here," Mia whispered. "You want me to leave and return to Villa Fabuloso."

"You're not a kid, Mia," I said. "You don't have to do anything you don't want to."

"What makes you think Nancy and I don't want to be renewed too?" Bess asked. "After you raved about Roland, we want to see what the buzz is all about."

Mia glared at us, then turned and huffed away.

"Something tells me she doesn't trust us," Bess said with a touch of sarcasm.

"Let's just hope Mia doesn't speak to Roland," I said. "Or Inge."

Then, as if my mind was being read, Inge's voice crackled over the PA system. She was telling guests that Roland would be speaking at ten p.m. sharp in the sanctuary.

"The meeting will include an orientation for all new guests," Inge said, "plus an evening meditation."

When Inge's broadcast was over, I said to Bess, "Roland is starting his lecture at ten? They really don't want us to sleep."

"Have another cup of swamp-water coffee," she said, sighing. "It's going to be a long night."

The sanctuary turned out to be the huge room at the top of the spiral staircase—the one with all the pillows strewn on the floor facing Roland's throne.

"Look, Ralph, there he is!" Linda squealed as we filed into the room.

"It's Roland, all right," Ralph said with a grin.

I could see the towheaded, tanned man from the portrait taking his place on the throne. Although everyone in the room was staring at him, he made no eye contact in return.

Bess and I lowered ourselves onto cushy pillows. I could smell the fresh flowers and scented candles flanking Roland's chair.

Daisy leaned over behind us and whispered, "Isn't he the picture of serenity and tranquility?"

And arrogance, I thought. But I smiled back at Daisy and whispered, "Totally."

Bess and I took our cues from the others, sitting cross-legged on our pillows. Mia was on a satiny pillow closest to the stage, her face turned up and smiling.

"Silence, everyone," Inge told the guests. "Silence, please."

When the room was quiet, Inge nodded at Roland to begin. I expected him to start speaking right away. Instead he turned his head slowly, making eye contact with everyone in the room, one by one. A shiver ran up my back as Roland gazed at me with pale blue eyes. Could he see right through me? Could he tell the reason I was here?

Stop it, Nancy, I told myself. *This guy has no special powers. He just wants us to think he does.*

After Roland had stared down the last guest, he spoke. "Welcome, welcome. I would particularly like to greet all our new guests. Will they please raise their hands?"

Bess and I reluctantly raised our hands along with the other newbies.

"Friends, renewal is a miraculous process," Roland stated. "What could be more fulfilling than discarding old habits and ways, embracing a new persona as if we were newly born?"

I could hear some guests murmur in agreement.

"But we cannot renew unless we know what we are renewing," Roland said. "So I would like for you all to meditate on what you would like to change in your lives."

Some guests shut their eyes in meditation almost immediately.

"And remember, I am not here to judge," Roland added. "Instead think of me as your trusty Sherpa, guiding you up the craggy but rewarding mountain of rebirth."

"What is he talking about?" Bess whispered.

"Just pretend to meditate," I whispered. "Close your eyes and think of Rodeo Drive."

"Gladly," she said dreamily.

I closed my own eyes but didn't imagine Rodeo Drive. I thought about what George was up to. Was she at her computer researching Roland and his retreat?

"Open your eyes slowly," Roland said softly. "Now, who would like to share their thoughts?"

Mia's hand shot up in the air. "I will," she said.

Roland grinned. "Tell us what you'd like to change in your life, Mia," he said.

Mia stood up and faced the others. "What I really hate is being stepped on like I was some doormat," she said angrily. "I'm sick of my sisters telling me that I'm plain and overweight and nothing but a drag!"

Wow, Mia was furious. She was about to continue when Bess shouted, "Your sisters don't mean it. Mandy and Mallory love you. They really do."

The room became dead silent. All eyes, including mine, were on Bess.

"Keep your thoughts to yourself," Brad snapped at Bess. "Unless Roland asks you to share them."

"Brad," Roland scolded. "Remember, no judgment. Especially among our new converts—I mean, guests."

Roland smiled at Bess and said, "Let's hear from our new friends. Would you like to go next?"

Bess smiled back, but from the corner of her mouth whispered, "Nancy, what do I do?"

"Make something up," I whispered back.

Bess stood up and cleared her throat.

"What I'd really like to change in my life is"—she paused—"my wardrobe! I know you're all thinking my clothes are pretty fashion-forward. Okay, thanks for that, but I've had some of these outfits for two years. Two years—can you imagine? That's practically vintage!"

Everyone stared at Bess in disbelief. I held back a

giggle as she turned to Roland and said, "So, what do you think?"

"Well." Roland was staring at Bess too. "If that's what you envision . . . the universe will provide."

I flashed Bess a thumbs-up as she sat down on her pillow. We both listened quietly as more guests stood up to share their hopes, fears, and insecurities. All the while I was wishing and hoping that Roland would not ask me. Fortunately, I was spared.

"Now that we all understand the renewal process—come! Come fire walk with me!" Roland said, jumping to his feet.

A few guests leaped to their feet and cheered. I turned to Bess and said, "Did he just say *fire walk*?"

"What is that?" Bess asked.

There was only one way to find out. We followed the others down the stairs, out to the beach. The first thing I saw was attendants lighting up a path of hot coals.

"Uh-oh," I murmured to Bess. "Is this what I think it is?"

While guests began lining up behind the glowing path, Inge made another announcement.

"For those who have never done this, listen carefully," she practically shouted. "As you take off your shoes and socks, you must prepare yourself mentally to walk over the coals."

"What?" Bess cried. "We have to walk *barefoot*?"

Roland stood at the end of the path. "If you commit to the challenges here at the retreat, you commit to the renewal process too," he said.

I could see Daisy quickly slipping out of her sandals. But Terrence pulled off his sneakers and socks reluctantly.

"Fire walking is an ancient ritual," Bess said. "I think the Native Americans practiced it."

"I'm sure the Native Americans knew what they were doing," I hissed. "I'm sure Roland does not!"

"Start taking off your shoes, girls," Inge told us. "You must be ready when your turn comes."

I could smell the smoke, hear the sizzle, and see red-hot embers shoot into the air. This was insane!

"Don't even think of doing this, Nancy," Bess whispered. "We can get seriously hurt."

"Bess," I said slowly, "if we refuse to do these challenges, we'll get kicked out of the retreat before we can find out what's really going on."

"Haven't we found out enough?" Bess whispered. "This place is nuts. Period. Let's pack."

"Girls!" Inge called to us. "I don't see you preparing."

"Nancy," Bess said as she dug her nails into my arm. "What are we going to do?"

IDENTITY REVEALED

"We're not walking forward," I told Bess. "Stall as much as you can while I think of a way out."

The first person to fire walk was Mia. She waved her arms in the air as she scurried across the glowing coals. Roland and the others were cheering so loudly I couldn't tell if Mia was screaming or not.

At the end of the path, Roland greeted Mia with a big hug. I wanted to barf.

"Ralph, you're next!" Roland said with an excited little hop.

Ralph stood barefoot. "Bring it on!" he shouted.

"Go, Ralphie! Go, Ralphie!" Linda chanted as her husband sprinted from one end to the other.

"Ralph's feet don't seem to be burned. Neither were Mia's. Do you think there's some scientific reason no one is getting hurt?" Bess asked me.

"If there is," I said, "this is one experiment I'm not willing to conduct."

Terrence had slipped behind us at the back of the line. "I know Daisy is really into this," he said. "But I think it's nuts."

I was about to agree when an earsplitting shriek filled the air. Danielle collapsed on the sand. She was on her back, clutching her left foot.

"Owww! I burned my foot!" she wailed.

I glared at Roland as Bess and I hurried over to her. "Sizzling hot coals have a way of doing that," I said angrily.

"Danielle will be fine. All she needs is a little cold water," Roland said.

"What she needs is an emergency room," Bess insisted. "Nancy and I can drive her to the hospital—"

"Absolutely not!" Inge interrupted. "We have perfectly good natural remedies right here at the retreat."

It was déjà vu. Inge had repeated almost exactly what she'd said in the emergency room—when she'd kept Brad from getting medical help the day before.

Now she was doing the same with poor Danielle.

Too stunned to speak, Bess and I watched as two attendants helped Danielle to her feet, or at least the one that wasn't injured.

Roland remained eerily calm. "Girls? Would you like to rejoin the line so we can complete the challenge?" he asked Bess and me.

I no longer needed an excuse.

"After what happened to Danielle," I told Roland, "I'd rather not go through with the challenge."

"Me neither," Bess agreed.

Roland glared at us.

That's it, I thought. *Any second Roland and Inge are going to demand that we leave the retreat. And we'll never know the truth.*

Amazingly, he smiled.

"This is only your first day," Roland told us. "Resistance is perfectly normal."

"It is?" I asked, not knowing what else to say.

"Of course," Roland said. "By admitting your reluctance with total honesty, you both have passed the challenge."

"Everybody return to your rooms," Inge shouted. "There will be a quiz on chapter seven in Roland's book tomorrow."

"A nonjudgmental quiz!" Roland added.

"At least we got out of fire walking, Bess," I said as

we trudged back to the mansion. "Not that we'd ever do it in the first place."

"I hope Danielle gets the attention she needs," Bess said with a sigh.

The others were filing through the door into the mansion. Bess and I were about to follow when I noticed something on the side of the entrance— a pile of white plastic bags. When I took a whiff, I knew what was inside.

"Garbage bags," I said. "What are they doing on the beach side of the house?"

Bess looked from the bags to the ocean. "So they can load it onto the yacht and dump it into the ocean?" she asked. "Do you still believe that, Nancy?"

"As detectives, we have to consider all options," I said. I pulled out my phone and snapped a picture of the bags. "As soon as we get to our room, I'll send this evidence to George."

"What?" Bess teased. "You're not going to read chapter seven in Roland's book?"

"Maybe I will," I teased back. "After what happened on the beach, I'll need something to help me sleep."

It was way after midnight by the time Bess and I got to bed. We were so exhausted that we practically passed out on the bare mattresses.

We slept for a total of three and a half hours before we walked into the dining room the next morning.

The other guests looked equally exhausted. I read what was on the breakfast menu: sugar-coated cereal, glazed doughnuts, and hot chocolate.

As Bess and I sat at a table, I noticed something else: Band-Aids on the upper parts of everyone's arms.

"Excuse me," I asked Daisy. "What are the Band-Aids for?"

"Vitamin shots," she answered.

In the seat beside her was Terrence, his eyes glassy and his voice flat as he said, "Why don't you sit with us?"

"No, thanks, Terrence. Bess and I want to . . . um . . . quiz each other on chapter seven of Roland's book," I told him.

Bess and I found an empty table.

"Vitamin shots, as if," I whispered.

"They're probably getting pumped with that sodium pentothal George told us about," Bess said. "Did you see how loopy Terrence was?"

"Yeah, but Daisy was okay," I said.

The sudden crackle of the PA system made us jump.

"Good morning," Inge's voice greeted everyone. "After breakfast we will gather on the beach for mediation and visualization."

"Sounds harmless," Bess said. "As long as we don't have to sit on burning coals."

After finishing breakfast, we picked up yoga mats

and headed to the beach. The white trash bags were still stacked near the door and smelled even worse.

"Find a spot to place your mats, girls," Roland called to us. "Then close your eyes and let your thoughts drift."

The other guests were already meditating. Instead of a rubber mat, Roland sat on a Persian-style rug trimmed with golden tassels.

I led Bess to the bushes separating the retreat's beach from ours.

"Why do you want to sit here?" Bess asked.

We began unrolling our mats. "I texted George on the way out and told her to meet us here," I said. "Let's see if she found out anything."

"I hope no one saw you use your phone," Bess said.

I shut my eyes and took a deep breath. A little meditation and relaxation couldn't hurt, especially after the last few days. But just as my thoughts began drifting . . .

"Psst."

My left eye snapped open. I turned my head to see George behind the bushes.

"How long have you been there?" I whispered.

"Just got here," George said, kneeling on the sand. "There was no garbage on our beach this morning. But wait until you hear the trash I dug up on Roland."

I made sure Roland's and Inge's eyes were shut. "Go ahead," I whispered to George.

"Roland has a criminal record," she replied. "His real name is Marty Malone, and he was arrested for embezzlement a few years ago."

I remembered my father once explaining embezzlement to me. It was the crime of stealing money or property from an employer, a company, or the government. Pretty serious stuff.

"Roland owned a real estate agency in San Francisco," George went on. "He stole money from his clients and his employees."

Bess had wiggled closer to the shrub to listen. "No way! I wonder how he resurfaced as 'Roland,'" she said.

"I don't know, but this guy sounds nuts," George said. "Why don't you come back to the house before things go too far? Mia is an adult. She can look after herself."

I shook my head. "We're already onto something," I said. "Roland is endangering his followers and injecting them with 'vitamin' shots."

"Which is probably that drug you told us about," Bess added.

"Ladies?" a voice called. Roland looked disapprovingly at us.

"Talking does not help the renewal process," he said. "Please continue to meditate silently."

George ducked, and Bess and I quickly shut our eyes. All I could see was the face of Roland—or Marty Malone.

So Roland is a criminal, I thought. *Why am I not surprised?*

"We survived meditation," Bess said as we climbed up the spiral staircase a few hours later. "What's next?"

"Something called Confrontation Celebration," I replied. "I heard Brad and Danielle mention it on the way in."

But when we followed the other guests to a small room off the sanctuary, my stomach did a triple flip. It was the same room those horrific insults had come from.

"I think I just figured out what Confrontation Celebration is," I told Bess as we entered the room.

Inge directed us to a semicircle of chairs facing Roland. Once we were seated, he spoke. "If you are going to abandon your old self, you must know what you are about to give up."

I looked at Bess from the corner of my eye. Hadn't we just done this?

"Daisy, stand up, please," Roland said. "Tell the group what you would like to change about yourself."

Daisy stood up and grinned. "Oh, wow!" she said.

"I eat way too many red velvet cupcakes, but the ones at the bakery down the block from me are so incredibly good that I can't resist."

"What word do we use for people like Daisy?" Roland asked.

Bess raised her hand. "Foodie?"

Brad sneered. "More like a gluttonous, disgusting pig! *Oink, oink, oink!*"

Omigod! Soon everyone—except us—was shouting, "Fat, disgusting pig! Pig! Pig! Oink, oink!"

Horrified, I looked at Daisy. Her face turned bright red. She started to shake and looked on the verge of tears.

Suddenly Bess called out, "Next!" She jumped to her feet and placed her hand on my shoulder to gently push me back into my seat. "Okay, let's see. What don't I like about myself?"

Everyone waited until Bess snapped her fingers and said, "I know. I can be too girly sometimes. You know, a lot of pink and ruffles and glitter."

"In other words, you're a shallow, vapid *loser!*" Roland said, emphasizing the last word.

"Loser! Loser! Loser!" the others chorused before Bess could reply.

I looked up at Bess. She seemed to be taking it amazingly well. She smiled and nodded at the insults being hurled.

"Thanks, you guys," Bess said when the shouting was over. "I feel better already."

"You were able to take that?" I whispered after Bess sat down.

"Sure." She shrugged. "Look who's saying it, Nancy—*Roland*!"

But Daisy wasn't doing so great. I could see her hanging her head.

Oh, help, I thought. *When will this be over?*

After each guest had been "confronted," Roland spoke again.

"All the new members have passed our most difficult challenges," he declared. "So everyone in this room is ready to board the Renewal Cruise." Cheers filled the room. He continued, "We'll sail tonight at seven o'clock sharp."

As we left the room, the others chatted about the cruise.

"I've been on a Renewal Cruise before," Danielle said.

"Is it on the yacht?" I asked.

Danielle nodded. "There's food, music, meditation, and personal growth exercises."

"What does that mean?" Bess asked.

"You'll find out," Danielle said with a tiny smile.

She hobbled away to the dining room for lunch, her foot still injured.

"Food, music," I said quietly. "And. . . garbage?"

"Do you think we'll be sailing with those bags?" Bess asked.

"As Danielle said, we'll find out," I replied. "In the meantime, let's see if that garbage is still outside."

We passed the spa rooms on our way outside. Instead of garbage, I smelled scented candles and fresh flowers.

"Oh, wow. Look!" Bess said. She pointed to a door marked SPRAY-TANNING BOOTH. "I always wanted to see one of those."

We stepped inside the unattended room and looked around. The spray-tanning booth wasn't hard to find. It was a huge glass cylinder with a sliding door. The glass was frosted blue, making it privately opaque.

"These are practically retro," Bess explained. "Nowadays most people get tanned with handheld sprayers."

"How does it work?" I asked.

"The spray nozzles must be inside," Bess said. She slid the door open and stepped inside. "Let's check it out. There's room for two in here."

"You want me to go inside there?" I asked. "What if it starts to spray?"

"The controls are on the *outside*," Bess said. "Come on, Nancy. Hurry up and get in!"

I could see the controls Bess was talking about. "Okay," I finally said, and went inside. "But let's make it fast, before a Lotus or Ivy or Cinnamon shows up. We don't want to get kicked out of the retreat."

Bess turned slowly, checking out the apparatus.

"Those must be the nozzles," she said, pointing to what looked like regular shower nozzles. "I think they move up and down as they spray, so they get every part of your—"

SLAM!

A light flashed on as Bess and I whirled around. The glass door had slid shut. Bess grabbed the handle on the inside and gave it a pull.

"Great!" she grunted as she tugged at the handle. "The door won't open. Now what do we do?"

I was about to call for help when I heard a loud *WHOOOSH!*

Bess and I shrieked: Nozzles went off at us, spewing spray tan at full blast!

Without goggles to protect my eyes, I squeezed them shut. "Besssss!" I screamed. "Shut this thing off!"

"I don't know how!" she shouted back. I could hear her fists pounding on the door. "It's run from the *outside*, remember?"

"Great!" I cried above the whooshing noise. I started pounding on the booth too, shouting for help.

After about sixty seconds, the door slid open a

crack. I reached my arm out and opened it the whole way.

Bess and I tumbled out of the booth. I gasped. We were covered in a slick, orangey spray from head to toe.

"Oh, no," I cried. "Look at us!"

I heard footsteps outside. I ran to the door and looked out—racing away was Mia Casabian!

"Mia, stop!" I called.

But she kept running. If I hadn't been so exhausted, I would have chased her.

"It was *Mia* who locked us in," I said as I went back into the room.

"Why would she do that?" Bess said, shaking her head. "She's supposed to be the sensible and nice Casabian."

"Because she's protecting Roland? *Or herself?* Mallory and Mandy were right when they said Mia's a different person. She's frightening," I answered. "Look at us. Our skin is ruined and so are our clothes."

"How did Mia even trap us?" Bess wondered, examining the sliding door. "There's no lock on the outside."

"She could have used this." I spotted a broom on the floor next to the booth and picked it up. I slid it through the door handle and tried to pull the door open.

"This does the trick," I said as I took the broom-stick out and leaned it against the booth.

"Was she *spying* on us?" Bess asked.

I nodded at the door and whispered, "Speaking of spies . . ."

Inge was standing in the doorway, her eyes burning.

"What are you doing in here?" she demanded. "The spa equipment is not to be handled by guests."

I was tempted to tell Inge that we'd been locked in the booth but changed my mind. For all we knew, she was in on it. We couldn't risk being kept from the cruise that night.

"Sorry," I said, shrugging. "We were just curious."

"I hope this stuff comes off," Bess said, raising a rust-colored arm.

My skin started to itch as Bess and I followed Inge down the hall. Amber, another employee, greeted us in a room equipped with showers and stainless-steel bathtubs.

"Too much of a good thing?" Amber asked.

"Don't ask," I said.

The moment Inge left, Amber got to work soak-ing and scrubbing us until just a slight trace of the orangey film remained. Since our clothes were beyond repair, Amber presented us with complimen-tary "Roland's Renewal" T-shirts and shorts.

"Let's go to our rooms and change for the cruise,"

122

I told Bess. "The last thing I want to wear is this scary logo."

We didn't get far.

Cinnamon was blocking the door, a tray in her hands.

No doughnuts or soda here.

Instead, smack in the middle of the tray were hypodermic needles!

Two of them.

HIGH-SEA SLEUTHS

"Hello, girls," Cinnamon said, grinning. "I have your high-energy vitamin serum."

"I thought you were a manicurist," I said, my eyes still on the needles.

"I do whatever Roland asks me to do," Cinnamon replied.

Bess and I traded a glance. The spa in the front *was* a setup for the retreat in the west wing.

Cinnamon lifted the tray. "Who's first?" she asked.

I knew Bess was thinking exactly what I was. *How do we avoid those shots?*

"Thanks, Cinnamon." I smiled. "We already had our vitamins this morning."

"It didn't say that on your charts," Cinnamon said, taking another step forward.

"Actually, we're phobic," I blurted. "Can we please see how long the needles are before we take the shots?"

"I suppose." Cinnamon shrugged.

As I leaned over to study them, my arm "accidentally" knocked the tray out of her hands.

"Oh, no!" Cinnamon cried after the needles had clattered onto the floor. "They were sterile until now."

"Later!" Bess said to Cinnamon with a little wave. "Nancy and I have to change for the cruise."

We shot past her and practically ran to our rooms. Once inside, Bess flopped back on her bed and stared at the ceiling.

"That was close," she said. "What about the others? Shouldn't we tell Mandy and Mallory that their sister is being injected with that drug?"

"Not yet," I said. "We'll contact the police when the time is right."

"Nancy, if we don't get the police here soon, we'll *never* help Mia or the others," Bess said.

"Roland is a pro. He'll just trick the police into thinking this is a harmless self-help spa."

"I guess," Bess said.

"That's why the garbage bags with the needles are vital," I said. "If we can get evidence that the retreat is dumping trash in the ocean, it'll blow the whistle on everything else in this place."

Bess closed her eyes to take a rest. I texted George, telling her about the cruise. She answered immediately: IF U NEED ME SOS!

I was about to rest myself when there was a knock on our door. Bess sat straight up.

"Who is it?" I called.

"It's me, Daisy," a soft voice replied.

Bess got up and opened the door. Daisy's face was pale and her hair disheveled.

"Come on in," Bess said, whisking her into the room and shutting the door. "Are you okay? I hate to say it, but you look awful."

"I know, I know." Daisy sighed as she sat down on my bed. "We just had the most awful workshop."

"Workshop?" I asked, sitting next to her.

"Roland had a table covered with the most awesome-looking chocolates," Daisy explained. "And me being such a foodie—I mean pig—I couldn't wait to try some."

"Sounds like fun to me," Bess said.

"Not exactly," Daisy said. "I bit into a chocolate and thought I'd die. They were filled with wasabi and jalapeno peppers!"

"Are you serious?" Bess cried.

"I hope you spit it out, Daisy," I said.

"Roland wouldn't let us. He kept shouting at us to feel the fire in our bellies. All I could feel was the fire in my mouth," Daisy said.

I placed my arm around Daisy's shoulder. Another crazy and dangerous workshop led by Roland.

"I know I was a Roland worshipper when I got here," Daisy admitted. "But I don't want to be around him anymore. All I want to do is go home."

I was glad that Daisy was coming to her senses. But there was still something I didn't get.

"Why did you come to us?" I asked.

"I could tell you weren't crazy about the place either," Daisy explained. "Will you leave the retreat with me?"

I wished Bess and I could leave, but we couldn't. We also couldn't tell Daisy the real reason we were here. "We're going to stay until the end of the program, Daisy," I said gently. "But don't let that stop you."

"Yeah," Bess agreed. "Just pack your things, go downstairs, and leave."

"The retreat took my money when I got here." Daisy sighed. "How will I get home? My mom lives in Denver."

I didn't think Bess and I could help Daisy in any way. Then I had an idea.

"Daisy, go the house next door and introduce yourself to George," I said.

"George?" Daisy repeated. "Is he your brother? Boyfriend?"

Bess giggled and said, "George is a girl. Her real name is Georgia—but don't tell her I told you."

"George will let you call your mom so you can arrange a way home," I explained. "You can stay with her until you figure something out."

I pulled out my phone and found a picture of George. "Here." I showed it to Daisy. "This is what she looks like. I'll text her to let her know you're coming."

"You have a phone in here?" Daisy gasped. "I thought we weren't allowed to have phones."

"Let's just say we beat the system," I said with a smile.

"Thanks, you guys!" Daisy exclaimed. She hugged both Bess and me. "I'll sneak out before the cruise."

"Wait a minute," I said as Daisy headed toward the door. "What about your friend Terrence? Doesn't he want to go with you?"

"Terrence suddenly likes this lame retreat," Daisy said sadly. "Go figure."

As Daisy slipped out of the room I whispered, "Good luck."

I texted George to give her the heads-up on Daisy. WHAT ABOUT MIA? George texted back. BRAINWASHED, was all I replied.

At least Daisy was being rescued. I looked up from my phone and smiled. "One down. Now let's get ready for that mystery cruise."

"Glad you could make it!" Roland said as he greeted everyone on the beach. He was standing about ten feet away from the big covered tent, wearing khaki shorts, a Hawaiian aloha shirt, and a shiny silver admiral's whistle around his neck.

In their island wear, Ralph and Linda resembled the Howells from *Gilligan's Island*. It was hard to tell if the couple was loopy from "vitamin" injections or just being themselves.

Roland began checking names on a clipboard. For the first time since we began the program, Terrence was standing alone.

"I'm glad Daisy got away," I pointed out. "But poor Terrence."

Roland grinned as we made our way to him and his clipboard. "Nancy and Bess." He checked our names off with a flourish. "Check . . . and check. Enjoy the cruise, you two."

"Thanks," was all I could say.

As we walked away from Roland, Bess whispered, "I don't see Mia anywhere, or the trash bags."

"What happened to them?" I wondered.

Just then someone called our names.

We turned to see Mia, heading over to Roland. She smiled slyly at us and said, "Nice tans."

"Ignore her, Bess," I whispered. "Let her think that we've fallen under Roland's spell too."

I felt my phone vibrate in my jacket pocket. "There goes my phone," I whispered. "Stay here while I take it."

I ran all the way around the big tent. When I was sure I was hidden from the others, I pulled out my phone and read George's text: WHERE IS DAISY? NEVER SHOWED UP.

"Never showed up?" I said, staring at the message. Quickly I sent George a question mark.

Bess joined me behind the tent. I showed her George's text. "Maybe she got her money back from Roland and went home to Denver," she said.

But when we stepped out from behind the tent, I spotted Daisy walking alone on the beach.

"Daisy!" I called.

She turned to us, poker-faced, as we came running over.

"Why didn't you go next door to George?" I asked.

"I decided I wanted to stay here," Daisy answered flatly. "My renewal intensive has only begun."

Her voice was lifeless, and so were her eyes. What had happened to her since she came to our room?

"Daisy, you told us you didn't want to be around

Roland anymore," I said slowly. "He made you eat hot chili peppers. You said that was the last straw."

"I was just being resistant." Daisy shrugged. "Roland says it's natural and part of the renewal process."

"But—," I began to say.

"See you on the cruise," Daisy interrupted. She then turned away and walked toward Terrence.

"They got to her," I said. "Whether it was another injection or some other creepy method—this is trouble."

"Nancy," Bess said. "Daisy knows you have a phone and that you're connecting with George. What if she tells Roland or Inge?"

"Hopefully she's too spaced out to remember," I said.

The screech of Roland's whistle made Bess and me jump.

"All hands on deck!" Roland shouted. "Listen to Inge for instructions."

Inge briskly directed us to climb into three separate rowboats. Bess and I shared one with Brad and Danielle and an attendant working the oars.

"How's your foot, Danielle?" I asked as we began to drift toward the yacht.

Danielle glanced down at her foot, still bandaged. "Well," she said. "It's still a bit—"

"Couldn't be better," Brad cut in.

Bess and I traded a look that said, *Whatever.*

As we neared the yacht I caught a whiff of some-thing definitely not a cruise buffet. Bess screwed up her nose too.

"I think we just found those garbage bags," she whispered. "They're already loaded onto the yacht."

Roland's gleaming silver yacht was even more impressive close up. Over a hundred feet long, it looked like one of those luxury super-yachts.

"Hurry aboard, hurry aboard," Roland shouted to us from the hull. "We have lots of inner work to do."

As we climbed aboard, we were greeted by crew members wearing white jackets with the sunburst logo. We were also greeted by a table filled with cookies, soda, and chips.

"At least the bean dip has protein," Bess said.

Retro disco music blared from speakers as the yacht drifted gently out to sea. Lanterns strung across the deck created a colorful glow as the sun began to set in the distance.

"I can smell the garbage, but I don't see it," I said, my eyes darting around the deck. "Where do you think those bags are?"

"You know the old saying," Bess whispered. "Seek and ye shall find."

We tried not to look obvious as we searched the main deck. Somewhere near the bow I spotted a mound underneath a tarp. Making sure no one was around, I pulled it back. Underneath were, not trash bags, but about six steel drums marked DIESEL OIL, HIGHLY FLAMMABLE.

"Whoa," I said. "There must be hundreds of gallons of oil in those things."

"Why would Roland carry this much oil onboard?" Bess wondered. "A yacht this size must have a huge fuel tank."

"Maybe he's stocking up for a long journey at sea," I said, covering the drums. "Hopefully this cruise isn't it!"

We were about to keep on searching when the music suddenly stopped.

"Everybody!" Inge shouted. "It's time for Roland's inspirational message."

"Here we go again," Bess said as everyone sat cross-legged on the dance floor. Roland was seated on an elaborate wicker fan chair instead of on a velvet throne.

Once everybody was ready, Inge nodded with approval. She then walked off, leaving Roland to gaze out at us with his steely eyes. When he looked at me, I smiled over gritted teeth. I was actually happy when he finally spoke.

"Some of you have heard me talk about 'stinkin' thinkin'," Roland began. "It's the negative and damaging thoughts we choose to control our lives."

I could see Mia lean forward as she took in Roland's words. If we were lucky, Mia—and even

Daisy—wouldn't say anything about my phone. If either one did, we were toast!

"You know those thoughts," Roland said, his voice beginning to rise. "I'm too fat! I'm not rich enough! I don't have my own reality show! Garbage! Garbage! Garbage thinking!"

I could see others nodding as if they got it. Brad actually had tears streaming down his face.

"The time has come to take those nasty, horrible thoughts and kick 'em to the curb," Roland said as he rose to his feet.

An attendant wheeled a large canvas bin over to Roland. The bin was overflowing with white plastic bags!

"Bess, there they are," I whispered.

"Many of you know the drill, since we've done this before," Roland said, his eyes flashing with excitement. "Everyone, grab a white bag. Take it over to the railing, and when I give you the signal, spill the trash—and your negative insecurities— into the sea!"

"But Roland, won't we be polluting the ocean?" Ralph asked. There was a murmuring in the crowd.

"No," Roland answered. "These bags contain pure, organic materials that won't harm the waters. The dumping will purify your souls."

The others raced toward the bin. Bess and I were too stunned to move.

"Do you believe this?" Bess asked. "Roland is using the trash as a symbol for negative thinking."

"And we now know that's how the garbage got onto Stacey's beach," I said. "It was dumped off the yacht the night I heard those voices."

"Move it, you two," Brad shouted at us. "Get with the program!"

Bess and I stood and walked slowly toward the bin. Some people were already racing toward the railing with their bags.

"I'm going to try to record this insanity," I whispered.

"What should I do?" Bess asked. "I can't pollute the ocean—even if it's just one bag."

I saw Mia glaring at Bess and me.

"Pretend to go along with it," I whispered, nudging Bess toward the bin.

"Hurry, hurry, hurry!" Roland shouted as the other guests pulled bags from the bin. Some were already untying and emptying bags over the rails.

"Garbage in, garbage out!" they began to chant. "Garbage in, garbage out!"

Everything was so chaotic that no one saw me slip behind the cockpit. With my back to the wall, I pulled out my phone. I pressed record and carefully reached out my arm.

"And . . . action," I whispered to myself.

"Okay, everybody!" Roland shouted. "Release all

that negative energy. Garbage in, garbage out! Garbage in, garbage out!"

I couldn't see much of the action, but I could hear. And what I heard next was someone yelling, "Stop!!!"

The deck became silent. Still recording, I peeked out and saw Inge storming over to Roland.

"Yes, Inge?" Roland asked.

"I must speak to you privately. NOW," Inge said.

"Everyone, continue reflecting. We will be right back."

She took Roland by the sleeve and pulled him near to where I was hiding.

"You didn't tell me you had the trash loaded on the yacht," Inge hissed.

"I don't believe I have to tell you everything," Roland snapped.

"Roland, don't you remember what happened the last time we did this exercise?" Inge asked. "The trash washed up on Stacey Manning's beach."

I tried to keep my hand from shaking as I held the phone. Inge was admitting the whole thing, and I was getting it word for word!

"You were supposed to get the attendants to clean it up, but you never did," she went on.

"How was I supposed to know some girl would step on one of our needles?" Roland said.

Omigod! He was talking about George!

"Roland, this is a bad idea and you know it," Inge said. "The last thing we need is the police knocking on our door."

"The police?" Roland repeated.

After a beat he turned to the people at the rail and shouted, "Okay, change of plans, everyone. Return your bags to the bin. We'll do another exercise later."

Everyone except Bess looked disappointed as they carried their bags back to the bin. As I stepped out from behind the cockpit, I pressed the stop recording button.

"Done," I told myself.

I looked up from the phone.

My blood froze.

Staring straight at me—and my phone—was Mia!

UNSPEAKABLE ACTS

"I just hung up with my father. He's not well," I lied. But then I told the truth. "Family is really important to me," I said, and shot Mia a look that said, *Don't you dare* as I stuffed the phone into my jacket pocket. Mia narrowed her eyes at me before heading toward the bin.

"Well?" Bess said as she hurried over. "Did you record everything?"

"Mission accomplished, but Mia caught me in the act." I sighed.

"What if she tells Roland or Inge?" Bess asked.

"Let's hope she listened to me," I said, and patted

the pocket holding my phone. "This is the proof we need to go to the police."

When all the bags were in the bin, music pumped and everyone drifted to the dance floor and buffet table. Bess and I passed on the snacks.

"Not only am I sick of sugar and carbs," Bess said, "but who knows if Roland slipped something into the food or the drinks?"

We kept our eyes on Mia, watching to see if she would go to Roland. She was busy dancing with Terrence. So far so good.

After another hour or so, I could see the retreat coming up in the distance. The cruise was coming to an end.

"Everyone gather for a final meditation," Inge called out.

Bess and I rolled our eyes at each other as we took our place on the dance floor. Mia sat directly behind us as we pretended to meditate.

Will she still rat on us after we get back to the mansion? I wondered.

All the more reason for getting my phone to the police as soon as possible.

The yacht anchored, and rowboats were waiting below ready to ferry us back to shore.

"What now?" Bess whispered as we climbed together into a rowboat.

"We go straight to our room," I whispered back. "We'll pack our stuff, sneak back to our house, and call the police from there."

"What are you guys whispering about?" Brad demanded.

Bess stared zombielike at Brad. "Just what a fabulous cruise this was," she said.

"Roland rocks," I added robotically.

When the boat reached shore, Bess and I practically leaped out. On the way up the beach, we walked by the tent. Attendants were slipping in and out of the flap doorway. I was tempted to peek inside, but there was no time. We had to escape the retreat, and fast.

Once inside the mansion, Bess and I bolted upstairs. Without bothering to take off my jacket, I began stuffing my things into my duffel bag.

"Did you send the evidence to George?" Bess asked.

"I will now," I replied.

I reached into the pocket of my jacket. But all I could feel was a packet of mints and a crumpled bill. Did I put the phone in my other pocket? I jammed my hand into it, only to feel a balled-up tissue and nothing else.

"Nancy, what?" Bess asked, sensing my panic.

"I was sure I put my phone in my pocket," I said.

"You mean it's not there?" she squeaked. "But all the evidence is on it."

"Don't remind me!" I said.

Bess and I turned my pockets inside out. I even checked all five pockets on my jeans, but there was no phone. Anywhere!

"Maybe you dropped it on the beach somewhere," Bess said. "Or in the rowboat while you were climbing in and out."

My heart raced as I turned toward the door. "Come on," I said. "Let's retrace our steps."

It was already past midnight as Bess and I ran downstairs and shot out the back door. I expected the beach to be empty. Instead we saw people filing inside the covered tent—Ralph, Linda, Brad, and Mia.

"What's going on in there?" Bess wondered.

Mia was the last to slip inside the tent. That's when something clicked.

"Bess, Mia was sitting right behind me during meditation," I said. "She probably took my phone while my eyes were closed. Why is she waiting to show it to Roland and Inge? What's her plan?"

"I don't know," Bess said. "But if she has it, we have to get it back."

Bess and I sneaked up to the tent and slipped through the entrance. Once inside, I gasped. The temperature must have been over a hundred degrees!

I looked around and saw Ralph, Linda, Terrence, Daisy, Brad, Danielle, and Mia—all sitting on towels facing a pile of smooth black stones. Underneath the stones were flaming sticks and pieces of wood. The fire caused the stones to sizzle and smoke and heat up the tent like an airless oven. What was going on?

Mia was sitting on the opposite side of the tent. Her eyes were shut, and her face was beaded with sweat.

"Well, now!" Roland's voice said. "We weren't expecting you two to show up to our purification ceremony."

Roland and Inge were seated on opposite sides of the doorway. They were the only ones drinking from water bottles. Two retreat attendants stood near them, looking more like guards than friendly spa employees.

"How come we weren't invited?" I asked.

"We were going to invite you to our sweat lodge," Roland said, fanning himself with a straw fan. "You ran to the house before we could."

"Sweat lodge?" I repeated.

"It's like a sauna, Nancy," Bess told me. "We'll probably just sweat a little until it gets too hot."

"Stop talking," Inge commanded. She tossed us each a white towel. "Find an empty spot and sit down."

The heat was unbearable, but so was the thought of losing my phone. While everyone closed their eyes in meditation, Bess and I squeezed into a spot between Danielle and Mia.

"Hand it over, Mia," I demanded in a whisper.

"What?" Mia asked.

"Silence!" Roland called out.

Mia glared at me. She got up with her towel, marched to the opposite side of the tent, and sat next to Daisy.

"I know it's hot in here," Roland said. "But we must welcome the intense heat, as it draws the impurities from our bodies and minds."

Bess and I sat on our towels, ignoring Roland's sermon. By now the temperature was so high that everyone was sprawled on their towels, their faces glistening with sweat.

Ten minutes slogged by, but the sweltering heat and airless conditions made it feel like ten hours.

I watched Roland fan himself with one hand and chugalug water with the other. Water he wasn't sharing with the rest of the group.

"I can't take it anymore," I told Bess. "Forget my phone. I'm going to faint."

Bess needed no convincing. Her hair was plastered against her neck, and her skin was beaded with sweat. "Let's go," she rasped.

But as Bess and I stood up, Inge barked, "Where are you going?"

"To get some air," I answered. "Before we pass out."

"Whoa!" Roland said as he blocked the doorway. "I didn't take you two to be quitters."

As if they'd gotten a second wind, the others began chanting, "Quitters, quitters, quitters!"

"So we're quitters," Bess said wearily. "Who cares?"

I stared at Roland standing in front of the doorway like a Doberman.

"Move aside," I ordered. "Let us out."

"Don't you dare talk to me in that tone," Roland said through gritted teeth.

The two beefy retreat attendants made their way over. They took their place in front of Bess and me and crossed their arms.

"If I were you," one of them growled, "I'd sit right now."

"Or you won't get the full benefits of my renewal process," Roland said.

"Nancy," Bess whispered. She grabbed my arm to hold herself up. "The heat's really getting to me. I can hardly stand up."

"Hang in there," I told her. I tried to figure another way out, but the heat was making it hard to think.

Maybe we can crawl out from underneath the tarp, I thought as my eyes darted around the tent. *Unless they stop us from doing that, too.*

"Bess," I muttered as we made our way around the

hissing rocks. "When we get to the other side, we'll slip under the—"

"Somebody help!" Linda's voice interrupted. "Something's wrong with Ralph."

I turned to see Ralph lying on his back, gasping for breath. No longer flushed, his face had a sickly pallor.

"He's probably dehydrated, just like Brad was," I said. "Roland, give him some of your water."

Roland handed his water bottle not to me, but to one of his attendants. As if to mock me, the attendant splashed water onto the rocks, making them hiss and heat the tent even more.

"Creep," I said under my breath.

"Ralph is fine, everyone," Roland announced. "He's in a state of ecstasy. Just like Mia here."

Mia? When I looked at Mia, she too was lying on the towel, breathing heavily.

"You mean a state of emergency," I snapped. "Let us out so we can call an ambulance."

"And stop the purification ceremony?" Roland said. "Why don't you sit down and shut up . . . or you'll soon need an ambulance too."

I got the threat, but each breath seared my lungs, making it impossible to fight back or argue. I sank back down on my towel next to Bess, who was fading fast.

"We can't crawl under the tent," Bess managed to whisper. "The tarp's too close to the sand and way too heavy."

"Let's use our hands to dig some space," I whispered, my eyes fixed on Roland and Inge. "We'll have to dig behind our backs so no one sees us, okay?"

But when I looked at Bess, I knew she hadn't heard a word I said. She had collapsed against the tarp, her eyes shut, her face pale.

"Bess!" I gasped painfully.

I called her name over and over again.

It wasn't long before my voice began echoing inside my head, and everything around me became a blur.

RESCUE AND REVENGE

"**N**ancy!" I heard a voice shout my name. "Nancy, can you hear me?"

My eyes flew open to see George kneeling over me. Instead of answering, I took a huge, long gulp of cool early morning air. It was still dark as I lay on the beach, but I wasn't on a blanket or towel. I was lying faceup on an ambulance stretcher.

"Welcome back," an EMS worker said, smiling down at me as he adjusted my IV. "You had some serious heatstroke going on, but you should be just fine."

Heat stroke . . . the tent . . . Bess!

"Where's Bess?" I asked, trying to sit up. "Is she okay?"

George put her hand on my shoulder to keep me down. "Bess is going to be fine too," she said. "She's on her way to the hospital, which is where you're headed."

"How did we get out?" I asked.

"Me," George replied. "When you didn't text me after the cruise, I got worried. So I sneaked onto the retreat's beach. That's when I heard screaming coming from the tent."

"Screaming," I repeated, remembering Linda.

"I called the police, and they came right away," George said. "It's a good thing, too."

I heard Roland's voice and turned my head. The sinister guru was waving his arms in the air as he spoke to police officers.

"I told you, officers, it was nothing but an unfortunate accident," Roland was insisting. "I must have turned the heat up a bit too much. You know how these saunas can get."

I wasn't worried about Roland. I knew he would get what he deserved. But what about the others?

"How's Ralph?" I asked George. "And Mia? She was in pretty bad shape."

"If you mean that older guy, he was taken to the hospital too," George said, helping me to sit halfway. "As for Mia, see for yourself."

I looked to where George was pointing across the beach. Mandy and Mallory, wearing their usual four-inch heels, were stumbling after Mia, who was being carried away on a stretcher.

"We heard the police cars and came right away," Mandy was shouting after Mia.

"Sorry, Mia," Mallory said next. "This wasn't the makeover we had in mind. You're our sister, and we love you!"

As I watched them lift Mia into an ambulance, I remembered my phone.

"George," I said, feeling dizzy again. "I recorded Roland ordering everyone to dump trash into the ocean. But Mia has my phone. We've got to get it back."

"Calm down," George said with a hand on my shoulder again. "Mia doesn't have your phone."

"She doesn't?" I asked. "Then where—"

"Ta-daaa," George sang as she wiggled my phone in front of my face. "That girl Daisy gave it to me."

Daisy, of course! Bess and I were so busy suspecting Mia we had forgotten about her.

"Daisy knew I had a phone too," I said. "She must have been watching my every move on the yacht and was planning to rat on me after the sweat lodge."

"Well, she's had a change of heart," George said, and grinned.

"What do you mean?" I asked.

"Daisy was the first to escape the tent after you

passed out," George said. "She told me that you were right about this place all along."

"But . . . how did she know to give you my phone?" I asked.

"She recognized me from the picture you showed her," George said. She then frowned. "She called me . . . Georgia."

I smiled as I felt my stretcher being lifted. It was Daisy, not Mia, who'd taken my phone. But at least I had the phone and video footage of Roland and Inge and the trash dumping. And *that* would lead to a crackdown on Roland's Renewal Retreat and Spa!

Bess and I were in excellent hands at Malachite General, the same hospital that had treated George. We were released in the afternoon, but poor Ralph needed to stay for observation. Luckily, the police and ambulances had gotten to him in time to save him—thanks to George.

We said good-bye to Mia, who also needed another day or two in the hospital. The drugs Roland had given her were slowly leaving her system, and so was her anger.

"Another relaxing day in Malachite," George joked as she drove us back to the house. "If you ask me, we'll need a vacation after our vacation."

I sat in the passenger seat while Bess sat in the back. Our energy had returned, along with the color in our cheeks.

"At least I got to show the video to the police at the hospital," I pointed out. "They were pretty impressed when we told them we were detectives."

"I'm sure Roland wasn't thrilled," George said. "With the dumping of the needles, the sweat lodge, and more embezzlement charges, he'll end up in prison for sure."

"Talk about a renewed life!" Bess laughed.

I was happy to see our borrowed beach house in the distance. We stared out the window as George drove slowly past the retreat.

"Wow," she said. "Check out the news trucks. And cop cars."

"I'm not surprised," I said. "The police have plenty of evidence to arrest Roland and Inge."

George stopped the car in front of the retreat. Rolling down my window, I called, "Excuse me, Officer, but are you here for Roland?"

The police officer approached our car.

"Roland? You mean Marty Malone?" he said. "Yeah, we're here to bring him in. There's just one small problem."

"What?" I asked.

"He's not anywhere in the house," the officer said.

"His accomplice insists she doesn't know where he went."

George glowered. "You mean Inge?"

"That's her," the officer said. "But don't worry. We'll find him sooner or later."

"I hope so," I said. "Thanks, Officer."

George drove the car up our driveway. She held the doors open for Bess and me as we slowly got out of the car.

"What a pal!" I teased George.

"What a cuz!" Bess giggled.

Once inside the house, I saw another message on Stacey's phone.

"It *can't* be for us," Bess said. "We already spoke to our families back home."

"I don't think we have to worry about creepy messages anymore." I smiled as I pressed the play button.

"You have one message," the machine droned. Then we heard Stacey's voice saying, "Hi, girls. Guess what? I'll be coming home tomorrow. Alas, the event was canceled, but as they say, *c'est la vie*. Of course, you can still stick around if you want to. The more the merrier."

George deleted the message.

"We have over two weeks left of our vacation, but do we really want to stick around?" she asked. "I mean, after all that's happened?"

I gave it a thought. "I still love California, and we

did make friends with the Casabian sisters. But River Heights is starting to look awfully good to me."

"Especially since it's far away from Roland," Bess said. "Where do you think he went?"

"Who knows?" I shrugged. "I just hope the police—"

BOOOOOOM!!!!

Bess, George, and I jumped sky-high at the sudden explosion.

"What was that?" Bess gasped.

"I think it came from outside," I exclaimed. "Somewhere in the back."

We ran out on the deck and stared at the water. I could see what looked to be a fiery boat in the distance. The three of us raced to the beach. Police officers stood on the shore watching the boat too. With them, her hands in cuffs, was Inge.

"That's Roland's yacht!" Inge was crying. "He didn't want to be taken alive. He didn't want to be taken alive!"

"Roland set fire to his own yacht?" I gasped as we stared at the shooting flames.

"It's more than a fire," George said. "It looks like an explosion."

"Nancy, the oil drums we saw on the yacht," Bess reminded me. "Roland probably blew them up—along with the fuel tank!"

Blowing up the yacht didn't make sense to me. But then again, neither did Roland.

"He probably wanted to go out in a blaze of glory," I said with a sigh. "Literally."

"The yacht isn't all that Roland destroyed," George muttered. "Look what he did to our beach."

I saw rainbow-colored oil puddles drifting ashore and knew exactly what she meant.

"Oh, noooo," I cried.

All those oil drums plus the fuel tank meant hundreds of gallons of oil. The damage to the beach and its wildlife would be catastrophic!

"And we thought the trash was bad," I said.

"How am I going to explain this to Stacey when she gets back tomorrow?" George groaned.

"So this is our fault, isn't it?" Bess asked sadly. "I mean, we provoked Roland, and this was his revenge."

I looked out over the ocean. Soon the oil would reach our beach, turning the sugary-white sands a dusky black.

"I don't know if it's our fault or not," I admitted. "But something tells me we're not going back to River Heights . . . at least anytime soon."